Who Do You Trust?

A NOVEL ABOUT DECEIT AND REDEMPTION

By

Charles D. Patton

Notice

This is a work of fiction. Names, characters, places, and incidents either are the product of the author's imagination or are used fictitiously. No resemblance to actual persons (living or deceased), places, buildings, and products is intended or should be inferred.

Role of Artificial Intelligence (AI) in this book: I found OpenAI's ChatGPT and Google's Bard helpful, as I am dyslexic, in cleaning up, simplifying, organizing, and clarifying my writing and in finding or checking sources. I am responsible for the story, the selection of subjects, outlines, structure, initial draft, the ChatGPT prompts I used, opinions, intentions, proposals, the plot, the characters and all of the final writing.

CONTENTS

CHAPTER 1 WASHINGTON DC

I was just nine years old when two men dressed in somber black suits arrived at our doorstep. I caught my first glimpse of them through the frosted glass, their posture rigid, like soldiers at attention. My sister, with my brother and me peeking from behind, curiously opened the door and inquired about their purpose. The shorter of the two men uttered it, matter-of-factly, as if they were informing us of a mundane matter, such as a forgotten garden hose or a neighborhood garage sale: "Your parents have passed away." At that moment, I recall my sister's hand clutching the doorknob tightly and the distant rumble of a garbage truck compounding trash at the end of our driveway. The taller man swiftly turned his head, startled by the noise.

"Car accident," the shorter man added, yet the pause before he spoke seared a lasting memory into my consciousness. Back then, the grim news meant I would navigate my pre-teen and teenage years without parents, grappling with the accompanying emotions and intermittent loneliness accompanying such a loss. It would profoundly reshape my existence, leaving scars deeper than I could fathom. In the years to come, the dreadful news would revisit me sporadically, an indelible childhood nightmare.

Following our parents' demise, my sister Crystal, a decade our senior, assumed both mother and father roles, a challenging responsibility for all of us. My brother Kenny and I eagerly sought independence once we reached the legal age, eager to grant Crystal the chance to relish the remnants of her youth. Upon leaving home, Kenny and I drifted from one job to another while Crystal pursued an Education degree. From then on, we orbited each other like distant planets—occasionally drawing near but often traversing vast distances. We were all compelled to mature prematurely. As for our parents' tragic fate, we never broached the subject again, not amongst ourselves and not with anyone else. Nonetheless, that fateful day remained etched in our memories, and I realized I would only place my trust in my immediate family for the remainder of my life. Henceforth, like countless other young individuals, my journey centered on discovering my life's purpose, a quest I anticipated would prove daunting, if not insurmountable.

CHAPTER 2 WASHINGTON DC

Two decades later, on a cold, rainy March evening, I arrived at the Gaylord National Resort and Convention Center to meet my girlfriend, Amber, for a charity art auction. The entrance was swarmed with taxis and limousines, and the doorman, clad in a bright red brocade coat, dashed back and forth between the vehicles and the entrance, his umbrella occasionally flipping inside out in the gusty wind. Initially, I kept my umbrella closed, stepping into a deep puddle that drenched my shoes and cuffs. I quickly opened my umbrella and moved toward the door, where I noticed a nun exiting the taxi behind mine, alone and without an umbrella. I stepped back to offer her shelter without hesitation and escorted her to the door. She was tall and slender. Once we were beneath the canopy, she thanked me in a raspy voice, and we parted ways. Drenched, I darted inside, determined not to be drawn into any further Good Samaritan roles by my conscience.

In her typically assertive manner, Amber had insisted that I was to meet her at the massive three-tiered fountain in the hotel lobby, so I made my way in that direction.

My brother, who always was in the middle of trouble, had introduced me to Amber about a year and a half earlier. Conveniently, he neglected to mention until months later that he had dated Amber until about a year before introducing us. I never quite felt comfortable with that part of her past. I was meeting her at the event because she was coming straight from work while I was coming straight from the couch in my apartment.

As I walked toward our rendezvous point, I couldn't help but dwell on the fact that our relationship had been rocky for the past four weeks. Amber was eager to get married, and I wasn't ready. Though she never explicitly said it, I sensed that I didn't match many of the qualities she envisioned in her ideal husband. She disapproved of my career choices, which had been aimless up to that point. We also disagreed on various other issues, including our political views. I tended to straddle the center while her views leaned hard left. Despite the underlying tension in our relationship, my plan for the evening was to make the best of it and avoid conflicts. However, things would only partially unfold as I had hoped.

The typical Washington Elite attended this charity art auction, or as I liked to call them, the Washington "effete." The only reason I had agreed to attend was that I was on a quest to find some clue, idea, or opportunity that would lead me to my lifelong passion and the perfect career connection. Until that point in my life, I had drifted from one dead-end job to another. I had tried Georgetown University for a couple of years, but the student body didn't quite suit me. Having been a Boy Scout during my childhood, I briefly entertained the idea of teaching Outward Bound programs, but I abandoned that after just one summer of leading uncooperative youngsters through the wilderness.

Most of them were as disinterested in the program as I was. That job left me feeling like I was stuck in my early childhood. Finally, I joined the Army, which was a lot like the Boy Scouts and Outward Bound, only with older participants, stricter rules, and harsher consequences for rule violations. I earned the rank of sergeant, but the role grew tedious, and I disliked taking orders, especially as it seemed that the longer I served, the more nonsensical the orders became. The Army was my longest job, but re-enlisting was not an option. Since then, I had been hoping for inspiration to strike, but it had yet to happen. Now, I was seeking inspiration at an event I could barely tolerate, hoping for something to change, and unexpectedly, something did.

I reached our meeting point, the enormous fountain in the main entrance atrium, at around 7:45 PM, dressed uncomfortably in my ill-fitting, damp, rented tuxedo. I must have been lost in thought because I was startled when Amber appeared before me at 8:10 PM, fashionably late. She was adorned in one of those classic "little black dresses" that women always seem to have in their closets, a single strand of pink-hued pearls, and high-heeled black patent leather shoes. At that moment, she reminded me of my sister. It struck me odd that she wore black, considering her hair was a shiny chocolate brown; I thought a color matching her hair might have suited her better. But then again, what did a twenty-nine-year-old guy know about how a twenty-six-year-old woman should dress? We looked like a pair of mismatched penguins, with me standing at six feet two inches tall and her at a mere five feet one inch. Unfortunately, her expression didn't match her fashionable appearance.

"Jake, early as usual," she remarked with a hint of irritation, glancing at her watch.

"Wouldn't want to keep you waiting," I replied with my most charming smile, but she didn't return it. A dark cloud seemed to hang over her demeanor more and more often lately, and it didn't sit well with me. It was a shame because her moodiness detracted from her otherwise striking appearance. Despite her gloom, I was determined to make the evening enjoyable.

As I took her arm, I noticed a man rushing by, perspiration glistening on his face. He wore a disheveled tan suit and was underdressed for a black-tie event like this. For a moment, I entertained thoughts of a potential terrorist attack. Terrorists had targeted the Munich Olympics a decade earlier, and the United States' relations with radical groups in the Middle East had deteriorated steadily since then. My concern might have turned into action if he had been younger and appeared Middle Eastern. However, he looked quite ordinary, fair-skinned, and empty-handed, so I dismissed him, thinking he might be a bartender or a late-arriving waiter. In hindsight, I should have been more attentive.

Amber and I strolled peacefully through the crowd of guests, who represented the typical Washington elite – politicians, influential lobbyists, well-connected defense contractors, oil industry executives, and foreign dignitaries with diplomatic immunity. The lawyer-to-civilian ratio was probably at least three to one, another aspect of Washington that irked me – too many lawyers and not enough everyday people running the country. My negative mindset continued to color my perspective, distracting me from the event.

As we meandered through the maze of partitions in the expansive convention hall, the organizers had transformed the otherwise sterile, rectangular space into what resembled a city version of a corn maze. Much of the art to be auctioned was displayed on these partitions. We navigated through various art pieces, small stands, and tables while people lined up at portable bars, clamoring for their first of many cocktails for the evening. The event aimed to sell artworks, with a portion of the proceeds going to charity and the remainder to the artists. Years of encounters with slick salespeople had made me cynical, and I couldn't help but view the whole affair as a ploy to help struggling artists sell works that they would never otherwise sell, all while splitting the proceeds with a charity that seemed to spend a disproportionate amount on overhead. My jaded perspective on both the art world and my relationship with Amber was not helping me enjoy the evening, and I couldn't help but wonder if this negativity was stemming from something deeper within me.

Amber stopped in front of a mixed-media three-dimensional piece that captured the essence of everything I considered disgusting -- clashing colors, body parts not meant for public display and grotesque rearrangement of those body parts. The artist stood proudly beside her masterpiece, explaining its inspiration to an older couple whose faces were scrunched like prunes. I'm not sure what the black-haired, gypsy-like, Bohemian artist was trying to convey, but she interested me far more than her artwork and was put together better. She sported multi-colored parrot tattoos on both biceps, multi-location piercings, and black net stockings that traveled a long way before disappearing beneath her short black leather skirt. I forced myself to wander on, leaving Amber to listen to what had to be an exercise in rationalizing the irrational.

After walking ahead, past a few more "works of art," I looked back to check on Amber. She appeared to have fallen under the spell of an old, grey-bearded gentleman who must have been an Ambassador from some small Latin American country, based on the cluster of ribbons on his chest and a gold medallion hanging from a chain around his neck. I backtracked and sidled up to the pair to try to peel Amber away. She didn't peel easily, but I was finally able to move her along.

The crowd appeared to be that typical Washington melting pot of back-slapping, back-stabbing politicians, money-wielding lobbyists, glutted defense contractors, oil industry bigwigs, and foreign dignitaries with diplomatic immunity -- that unfettered right to break our laws without consequences. The ratio of lawyers to regular people had to be at least three to one, another thing that galled me about Washington -- too many damned lawyers and not enough average Joes running the country. My negative mindset continued to distort my attitude, distracting me.

Moseying along with Amber, among those who consider themselves important, I suddenly noticed something happening. A muscular, dark-skinned, dark-haired man carrying a metal briefcase was hurrying through the crowd on a determined beeline toward the man in the tan suit, the one we had seen earlier. The rumpled man stood alone, apart from the crowd, across the room. At an event like this, being so underdressed, the man should have stood out like a cornstalk in a soybean field. However, he was so nondescript and low-key that he nearly disappeared into the woodwork. When the dark-haired man got to the rumpled man, he first tried to get the man to take the silver case, but when the rumpled man balked, the dark-haired man forced the handle into the rumpled man's hand. He did so by forcing the man's fingers around the handle of the case, using the firm grip of one hand, while placing, with his free hand, a handcuff around the rumpled man's wrist, connected to a chain running from the case.

The dark-haired man then hurried to a side exit door, and as he stepped through, shots rang out from the other side of the door. Then, a single hand holding an automatic machine pistol came around that exit doorway and began firing into the room. The arm looked wiry and thin, like a woman's. Guests dove, scattered, and screamed. I pushed Amber to the floor and crouched over her. Bullets were sprayed around the room but seemed to be going over peoples' heads -- high, on purpose, either by incompetence or nerves. A couple of bullets smashed into the giant overhead chandeliers, showering some of the crowd with glass shards. To my surprise, several guests were armed, quickly drew weapons, and returned fire. Bullet holes peppered the door and surrounding wall. By that time, the arm was gone, and so was the shooter. The armed guests cautiously pursued the shooter down the hallway behind the door. Having moved to my left, I caught a brief glimpse through the doorway of the body of the dark-haired courier lying on the floor in a growing pool of bright red blood. I helped Amber to her feet. She seemed more perturbed at my holding her down like I had spoiled her party, than grateful that I might have saved her life. She stomped out of the room.

Soon, the armed guests returned to the main room. I read their return as a sign that the shooter had escaped. Then, I noticed that the man in the rumpled tan suit was now crumpled himself, lying on the floor in a pool of blood, still clutching the briefcase handle. As the shock wore off, I saw other guests cautiously rising from the floor and rushing out the door. The action was over, and Amber had left the room, so I checked on the rumpled man.

One of the armed men, calling over a walky-talky for an ambulance, rushed over to the rumpled man as I had.

A second armed man was visible through the side exit door, checking the courier, and he quickly signaled to the man standing next to me that the courier was expired. I felt for the rumpled man's pulse -- it was gone. Another agent yelled out for all to hear, "Don't worry; it's all over. We're secret service agents. We had no idea anything like this would happen. Please remain calm, wait outside this room, and do not leave until we interview you." He then walked over to where I was bending over the rumpled man and tried to pry the briefcase from his hand but soon discovered the handcuff. I then realized that the shooter from the stairwell only started shooting randomly over the crowd as a diversion after hitting their specific target. The man on the floor had three bullet holes clustered closely in his chest and one in the center of his forehead. Those were not random hits.

I bent down to get a closer look at the man. I noticed Amber waving me out of the room from the corner of my eye. Before I left, I saw a scrawl of blood on the floor. It looked like the letters "NWO," whatever NWO was. I couldn't imagine what the scrawl meant, but I figured that would be a good puzzle for the Secret Service. The agents standing around the man didn't appear to notice or didn't care about the scrawl. One agent even stepped on it, mostly obliterating it. His inattention to detail appeared unintentional, but I wasn't sure. That puzzle, if it survived, would fall under the purview of the team that would come to photograph the scene and remove the body. I was surprised by my interest in what happened, including its aftermath, and my coolness throughout. A prenatal idea began to form in my mind. I went to find Amber in the lobby.

Most other attendees, including artists and organizers, were pacing around, talking nervously and speculating about what had transpired. Amber was once again working the crowd. One man claimed to have overheard a conversation between two agents, suggesting that the man who had been shot had been involved in spying on the United States and that they were taking his body and the briefcase to Langley.

"That's odd," I mused to myself. "Langley is the CIA's headquarters, not the Secret Service's. Why would Secret Service agents transport the man's body and briefcase there? After all, the CIA is prohibited by law from operating within the United States, although I suspected they had their ways."

After two hours of agents collecting names, contact information, and witness accounts, they finally informed us that we were free to leave. I wasn't ready to go yet, as I found the situation fascinating.

A thought suddenly surfaced as I searched for Amber, assuming she was still mingling with the political crowd. It hit me like a linebacker blindsiding a quarterback: a career in the CIA. It seemed like something I could embrace. It offered a sense of teamwork, excitement, and the potential for diverse experiences over time. After gaining some investigative experience, I could even dig into the mystery of our parents' deaths. Excitedly, I intensified my search for Amber to share my revelation with her. I eventually found her conversing with a British lobbyist and pulled her aside.

"Hey, honey, I've figured it out," I said.

"What did you figure out now?" she asked.

"I've figured out what I want to do for a career," I replied.

Her face lit up noticeably. "Wow, that's great! What is it?"

"I want to become a CIA agent."

However, her enthusiasm quickly faded, and her mood darkened once more. It was clear that she loathed the idea.

"Are you crazy?" she exclaimed. "You'll be constantly on the move, possibly in danger. If you think that's the life that I want to be a part of, you're dead wrong. And think about it – if we ever had children and something happened to you, it would be a repeat of what you went through – losing your parents, just like when you were a kid."

Her last comment stung, momentarily causing doubt to creep in. But then I recalled how my sister had raised my brother and me during those difficult times. We had come out of it alive, mostly well-adjusted, and still on speaking terms, at least occasionally. Moreover, I wasn't married to Amber, had no immediate plans for marriage, and certainly hadn't considered having children anytime soon. So, I dismissed her concerns.

"Seriously, that's what I want to do," I affirmed.

"Well, if you're serious, then I wish you the best," she said, spinning on her heels and walking away. She added over her shoulder, "I want no part of that."

With a wave of her hand, she departed without looking back. I didn't see or hear from Amber again that evening and had no idea how she had gotten home. I assumed she took a taxi. As for me, my excitement lingered, even though I had forgotten to retrieve my umbrella.

I was aware that I would start at the bottom, much like an apprentice, but I believed that I could gradually progress into a challenging and fulfilling position with a variety of assignments. For the first time in a while, I felt genuinely content, believing I had found something that could hold my interest for the long term, or so I thought. I couldn't help but ponder the mysterious man in the rumpled suit. What had that been all about?

The morning after the charity event, I decided to visit Amber's apartment, apologize, and see if any hope was left for our relationship. I picked up some freshly made bagels and the Sunday paper and headed over early. I had a key, and the fact that she hadn't asked for it back suggested something. I let myself in and went to the kitchen counter to grind the French Dark Roast coffee, which I knew she loved. The floorboards creaked above me, indicating that she was awake. "She's up," I thought, setting out two cups. I grabbed a tray and assembled the bagels, steaming coffee, and newspaper before going to the stairs. I heard giggling from upstairs, which reminded me that Amber enjoyed old comedy movies. I smiled as I approached her bedroom door, struggling to balance the tray and turn the handle. But then I heard giggling again, only this time, it was deeper and gruff, not Amber's.

Not Amber? My heart sank. She was in bed with a guy. In bed with a guy! I stepped back, almost out of the room, and saw Amber clutching the bedsheets to her collarbones while some guy attempted to squeeze his skinny legs into his jeans. I stared at him, and he stared back at me. It was like looking in a mirror. "Hi, Bro," he said, smoothing his hair.

I was so shocked that my response was feeble. I set the tray on the dresser by the door before storming out, blurting, "God, I just can't trust anyone anymore." As a parting gesture, I picked up the bag of bagels and hurled it in their direction. It was a mild reaction, considering the circumstances. I should have been angrier, but for some reason, I didn't feel as upset as I thought I should. I also felt a strange sense of relief, realizing that, in this case, ending the relationship wouldn't be as difficult as I had feared.

Back home, I pulled my dusty old car out of my apartment building's garage, a car I rarely drove in the city, and hit the road with no particular destination in mind. I needed to clear my head. At first, I drove aimlessly, which was easy given the haphazard layout of the roads in DC. Eventually, I headed into Virginia, passed the Marine Corps Museum at Quantico, and even went as far as Colonial Williamsburg. I decided to turn back before reaching the Norfolk tunnel and headed north again. Somewhere in Yorktown, I stopped for lunch while pondering the state of my life.

Eventually, I concluded that my sister might be the only person who could understand my confusion and offer valuable advice. So, I drove to her house in Georgetown. It was a modest home, mortgage-free, thanks to the life insurance our parents had left us. I hadn't seen her or the house in a while, and truthfully, I mostly wanted to share the story of our brother Kenny's misdeeds with her, as she had always been a mother figure in our lives.

Arriving late in the afternoon, I rang the doorbell out of politeness, even though I still had a key to the house on my keychain. She answered the door and left it open for me to enter. She led me to the living room and settled onto the couch. I closed the door behind me and joined her.

"So, what's been going on with you lately?" she asked. "You look like you've been through quite a night."

I proceeded to recount the events involving Amber and our dear brother Kenny. She expressed her frustration with Kenny but didn't offer to take any drastic action, as I had half-heartedly hoped she might. I also shared my thoughts about the charity art fundraiser and my recent contemplation of my future.

"I've been thinking about a new career direction," I confessed.

"You don't even have a career, do you?" she inquired. "Why don't you consider going back to the Army? I'm sure they'd be glad to have you back and might even offer to send you to Officer Candidate School."

"That's not an option," I replied. "I can't handle that level of structure and authority."

"Everyone has to deal with structure and authority at some point in their lives," she reasoned. "It's a pervasive part of society unless you plan to buy or take over some remote island nation and declare yourself king or dictator."

"Even as a dictator, I'd probably have to deal with internal power struggles," I said. "But that's not what I had in mind. I was thinking about joining the CIA as a field agent."

Her reaction was explosive as if I had ignited a stick of dynamite. "Absolutely not," she exclaimed. "You're not going down that path. It's far too dangerous. You'd be sent to who knows where, and the government would disavow any knowledge of your existence if things went wrong in a foreign country. It's more perilous than the Army, and they probably have more structure and authority than you can imagine. Plus, you'd be working alone in a foreign land where you don't even speak the language. At least in the Army, you have comrades watching your back."

"Well," I said, undeterred, "I've decided. It's the only thing I want to do."

"Don't do it, please," she pleaded. After a brief pause, she added, "I know how stubborn you can be. Promise me you'll think this through thoroughly before making any commitments."

"I will, but I don't think it will make any difference," I replied, although I wasn't entirely sincere. My sister sensed that, too.

"They probably won't hire you without a background in accounting or law or fluency in several foreign languages," she continued. "All I can say is, if you were looking for my approval, you've come to the wrong place. I believe it's a terrible idea."

She walked to a drawer in her china cabinet and retrieved something from it.

"Here," she said, handing me a small cross. "Take this and wear it. If you somehow do join, maybe it'll offer you some protection. It's a cross I brought back from Assisi, Italy, from the Franciscans. Perhaps it'll keep you safe or prevent you from rash decisions."

I draped the wooden cross, about an inch and a half long, on a leather cord around my neck and tucked it inside my shirt. Then, it hit me.

"Wait," I said. "You went to Italy last year? How come I didn't know about that?"

She hesitated before responding. "Well, I went with someone I wasn't sure would turn into a long-term relationship. I didn't tell you or Kenny because I didn't want to field questions about him that I wasn't prepared to answer."

"Man," I said. "You were out of the country, and I had no idea. And you were with someone significant enough to travel with, and I didn't know about it. I guess I've been too absorbed in my world. Can we make more of an effort to stay in touch this year?"

"You can count on it," she assured me.

As I left her house, I overheard her muttering, "It'll never happen! So, find something else to do."

My decision was firm. I went home and submitted my application to the CIA.

CHAPTER 3 WASHINGTON DC

In a couple of weeks, I received a phone call inviting me to an interview with the CIA.

In another week and a half, I survived three more interviews and filled out dozens of forms, including everything I could remember about my past. In another week, I received a letter welcoming me to a final selection process.

Enclosed with the letter were an airline ticket to Flagstaff, Arizona, and a rental car reservation. Included with the tickets were directions to a remote area in Arizona near a town called Tusayan. I had no idea where that was or what lay ahead, but I was as excited as a kid at Christmas. Due to leaving in two days, I called my sister to tell her, but she didn't answer, so I left a simple message on her recorder for her to call me right away. I was already practicing keeping my involvement with a spy agency unspoken.

She hadn't called me back by morning, so I called her again. Still no answer. As it was the time when she would typically be teaching, I even tried calling her school. She had given me the number months back in case I needed to reach her during the day. They said she wasn't there but wouldn't give me further information. Beginning to worry, I drove to her house to make sure she was okay.

When I got there, I became concerned when I saw several days of newspapers scattered around her door. I knocked, and when I got no answer, I used my key to open the door. I brought the old newspapers inside and dropped them on her coffee table. The house was clean, and I found no sign of her having been there recently or hinting at where she might be. She still had clothes in her bedroom closet, her trash had been emptied, and nothing she left in the refrigerator looked like it would spoil soon.

While pondering in her living room, I noticed a scrapbook sitting on a bookshelf. I opened it and was surprised to see many travel photos. There were pictures of her in Rome and Paris with some guy I'd never seen or heard of. The photos had a small year printed along their edges. Because the years were different on two of the pictures, the last two years, I could tell they were from different trips. She kept this guy secret even though she had traveled with him at least twice. I also noticed that while the two of them appeared together in several photos, they showed no sign of a relationship. They were never holding hands, leaning on each other, or touching. It seemed like a strange relationship. Like she said, she wasn't that wild about the guy and just wanted a traveling companion. There was something about the guy that made me uncomfortable, but I couldn't put my finger on why. He was about her age, mid-thirties, and about six feet tall with very dark eyes, a full head of dark brown hair, and a skin tone like but different from Hispanic or Mediterranean. I didn't see him as her type; frankly, he looked a little creepy to me.

Seeing that she wasn't home, I convinced myself to stop worrying about her. I knew she was an independent, intelligent soul who had lived independently for years and could handle herself in tight situations. At the time, I had no idea how much my assessment of her would turn out to be incredibly understated. Believing she must be away for a few days, I left a note asking her to call me the first chance she got -- that I had some good news. The next day, I was on the plane to Arizona. I didn't hear from her before I left.

CHAPTER 4 TUSAYAN AZ

During my drive from Flagstaff to Tusayan, the beauty of the Arizona desert landscape reminded me of the old cowboy movies I had watched on TV as a kid. I wondered if a ghost town would suddenly materialize around the next bend in the road. To my surprise, the next turn revealed a sign announcing the entrance to the Kaibab National Forest. The scenery transformed into dense stands of pine, fir, and Aspen trees, offering breathtaking views. The faint, pleasant aroma of pine pitch from the surrounding forest wafted through the air, reminiscent of a high-quality car air freshener. I pondered why the CIA had chosen such a remote location for the interview process when it could have efficiently been conducted at Langley, close to home. At least they had advised me to wear shorts and a T-shirt due to the scorching heat, which was quickly over 90 degrees in the shade.

My concern grew as the directions led me to turn off Highway 180/64 onto a Forest Service road. I wondered if I was the target of a cruel joke, an elaborate initiation ritual, or an orienteering test like what I endured in the Army. Or it was merely a case of receiving wrong directions. Just then, I reached the crest of a hill and saw a large flat parking lot nestled in a swale below, teeming with cars and around a hundred other candidates. There was no sign of civilization except for a canal lined with massive granite rocks that extended about 300 yards to the east from the parking area, then curved around a bend and vanished behind thick pine trees.

As I exited my car, I could sense the widespread confusion among the other candidates. No one knew what to do next or where to go. I walked over to the edge of the canal, joining the crowd. The only noticeable detail was a small arrow etched onto one of the rocks, pointing down the channel. However, traversing the jagged granite terrain in the indicated direction would be demanding. The rocks were sharp-edged, far from the rounded boulders I had expected. I recalled a similar experience at Mt. Washington in New Hampshire, where scrambling over such terrain had been physically taxing.

My first instinct was to find an alternative route around the canal, but it became apparent that both sides were fenced in with chain-link fencing, each topped with razor wire. My only way forward was to navigate the rocks with no other options. I started across them, and soon, others began following suit. My concern grew as I worried, I might lead them into a perilous situation.

I was thoroughly exhausted after covering about 75 to 100 yards of treacherous terrain in the scorching heat. Some candidates had fallen and sustained injuries, while others assisted them, helping them advance or return, depending on their condition and determination. Two fellow candidates, an older man and a young woman, caught up with me, so I paused momentarily to take stock. The older gentleman, Jim Smith from Illinois, appeared to handle the rocky terrain easily, clearly possessing natural strength. The young woman, Abigail Anderson from Texas, was also in excellent shape but had a different build type.

"Hello, I'm Jake Rhodes from DC," I introduced myself.

"Howdy," Jim responded. "I'm Jim Smith from Illinois."

"I'm Abigail Anderson, and I hail from Texas," she added with a hint of a Texan twang.

"You must be accustomed to this heat," I commented.

"I've never quite gotten used to it, but I've spent time in the desert," Abigail replied.

While I appreciated her response, I focused primarily on the challenging rocks ahead.

"I'd love to hear more about that, but it seems we're on a mission here and need to keep moving," I urged.

We resumed our scramble, and I soon had a revelation. I was dressed lightly – light enough to swim across the canal. It would offer a cooler, faster route, and the intense heat would quickly dry my clothes once I emerged. I didn't know if the others could swim or if they would follow suit, but it seemed like the right choice for me. So, I took the plunge, and Abigail joined me. Jim, however, continued to navigate the rocks. His agility made it appear effortless, showcasing his natural strength.

As we rounded the bend in the canal, we noticed its termination about 150 yards ahead. On the shore stood various tethered animals, including horses, mules, and donkeys. An assortment of ropes, bridles, saddles, and harnessing gear hung from nearby tree limbs and across logs. As a city dweller, I did not know which equipment matched which animal. In the distance, atop a series of ravines, ditches, and ridges, a large building resembling a conference center was nestled halfway up a mountainside, surrounded by towering pine trees. I deduced that we were facing the second part of an overarching challenge, and the next step was to determine how we'd travel from our current location to the building. But the mode of transportation remained a mystery to me.

By this time, Jim Smith had caught up with us after finally opting to swim across the canal. To my surprise, none accompanied him other than the eccentric tattooed artist I had encountered at the Black-Tie event, the one with the grotesque three-dimensional mixed media creation.

"Abigail and Jake, meet Jenny Jubilee," Jim introduced.

"I remember you," Jenny said to me. "You were at the Charity Art event a couple of months ago with that auburn-haired lady named Amber."

"She has an exceptional memory," Jim remarked. "And apparently, she can read lips."

"I was deaf for two years during my childhood," Jenny explained.

"That might be useful in this line of work," I commented. "Speaking of our mission, we need to select some animals and figure out how to get from here to there." I pointed in the direction of the distant building. "Any suggestions on which animals would be best and how to equip them?"

"I grew up on a farm," Jim replied. "Based on what I see, I think donkeys might be our best option."

"But aren't donkeys the slowest choice?" Jenny inquired.

"It all depends on how you define speed," Jim replied, beginning to craft a basic rope halter for the donkeys.

He meticulously prepared four of them, and it was fortunate that he did so as a horde of other candidates began to arrive and lay claim to their preferred animals and gear. Donkeys swiftly became a rare commodity, prompting our heavy reliance on Jim at this juncture. Jim expedited the mobilization of his chosen mount, and, fortunately, mine seamlessly followed his lead, with the other two falling in line behind mine. Meanwhile, other candidates were left floundering as they grappled with harnessing, saddling, or controlling their steeds. Those saddled with mules faced the most daunting challenge; these stubborn creatures pulled, bit, and even resorted to sitting down. In contrast, the horses displayed cooperation, but only for those with the knowledge to properly cinch a saddle. A few unfortunate souls fell off when the saddle slipped beneath their horse's belly, while others who managed to secure their saddles found themselves mercilessly bucked around, a harrowing experience for novice riders.

Once we surmounted the initial incline, Jim's choice was a stroke of brilliance. The rocky trail cascaded steeply downhill, weaving through several switchbacks before ascending again, with even more treacherous turns. Horses and mules, however, were forced to take a much longer route, veering widely to the right. Our chosen mode of transport was neither swift nor comfortable, yet it proved to be the most direct, catapulting us ahead of the competition. If the speed of our arrival constituted a test of our worthiness, then the four of us were excelling.

After forty-five grueling minutes, we reached our destination, dismounting our trusty steeds and tethering them to nearby fence posts. I was the first to enter the expansive hall, again greeted by a bewildering tableau. The hall resembled a vast convention center but with a more open layout. Confoundingly, no one was present to provide guidance or instructions. Stretching before us were booths and stations adorned with enigmatic and perplexing objects. Approaching the nearest table, I discovered an assortment of items resembling intricately braided fiber optics bundles. Each bundle boasted a unique pattern of strands, each adorned with minuscule fiber balls at its end, resembling diminutive nodules. These peculiar creations stood upright, resembling spiders perched upon spindly legs. Contemplating their purpose confounded me until I discerned an irregular pattern of small holes adorning the wall behind the table. It became apparent that I was meant to select one of these fiber optic devices and locate the corresponding openings in the wall. A sudden revelation struck me as I scrutinized the wall and the device in my grasp: a matching pattern amidst the wall's perforations. I approached and secured the device against the wall, skillfully aligning the miniature balls with the holes. The result was a dazzling display as the device illuminated like a radiant Christmas ornament. At that very moment, Abigail approached, but to my disappointment, the device abruptly extinguished, depleted of its brilliance. I discarded it in a conveniently placed trash can next to the table.

"Try one," I encouraged her. She selected a device yet struggled to discern a matching set of openings, suggesting that the task grew progressively more challenging. As she continued her efforts alongside Jim and Jenny, I moved on to the next station.

The subsequent station hosted an array of water guns, varying in shape and size. Other applicants had arrived and commenced an impromptu water fight, relishing the cool respite offered by the refreshing spray after scrambling over the rocky terrain. A few candidates who had opted for transportation other than donkeys had yet to arrive. However, one individual decided to elevate the aquatic skirmish by seizing a fire hose from a wall-mounted case. He brazenly unleashed torrents of water upon everyone, believing himself to be innovative and astute. I perceived his actions as unjust, almost bullying, prompting me to intervene. With swift motion, I disarmed him, relieving him of the hose, and retaliated with a controlled deluge. The forceful cascade of water swiftly subdued him, causing him to raise his hands in surrender. I deactivated the hose, pivoted, and was taken aback when I observed him charging toward me with his head lowered as if intending to drive me against the nearby wall. My reaction was instinctive as I elegantly sidestepped, allowing him to collide with the wall, rendering himself unconscious. My intervention garnered a modest ovation from fellow candidates whom his antics had tormented.

Progressing along the hallway, I encountered the subsequent station, which featured an assortment of specialized tools and an array of mechanical devices in various states of disrepair. Among these relics were a computer, a car engine, a boat motor, a diminutive steam engine, a model airplane engine, a vacuum cleaner, and numerous others. My attention was drawn to a small automobile engine mounted on a stand. An initial inspection revealed that the cylinder head had been fitted with a fresh gasket but with bolts that were inadequately tightened. I seized a torque wrench and approached the engine, finding a Haynes Service manual positioned nearby, tailored for the task at hand. Consulting the manual, I swiftly determined the correct torque specifications and methodically tightened the bolts. With the job accomplished, I returned the tool to its designated location on the table and transitioned to the next station, delegating the remaining responsibilities to subsequent candidates.

As I progressed through the perplexing series of exercises, I grappled with the significance of each station. My mind contemplated whether they constituted miniature tests designed to assess diverse skills encompassing dexterity, creativity, mechanical aptitude, curiosity, or leadership. Were these trials seeking individuals of exceptional ingenuity? The purpose behind the water guns remained an enigma, leaving me to ponder their mechanical relevance. My contemplations persisted as I moved forward while witnessing an influx of additional applicants converging upon the hall. Jim, Abigail, and Jenny diligently pursued the challenges, steadily closing the gap.

The subsequent area presented an open expanse adorned with several amusement rides. Two individuals sidled up beside me: one, a diminutive man with dark hair and a perpetual five o'clock shadow, who I later discovered to be older than he appeared; the other, a stereotypical tech enthusiast, sporting a pocket protector, horn-rimmed glasses, and high-top gym shoes. I examined the rides, attempting to decipher any potential relevance.

"What are your thoughts?" inquired the diminutive man.

"I'm at a loss," I admitted.

"It's roughly five-fifteen," remarked the tech enthusiast. "I wonder how long we're expected to partake in this."

"I'm unable to discern whether this is a timed trial, an accuracy assessment, a training exercise necessitating mastery at each station, or perhaps a test of our various skills," I mused aloud. "Do any of you have any insights?"

Both shook their heads, signaling their lack of clarity. I introduced myself, "I'm Jake Rhodes, the 'h' is after the 'R.'"

"I'm Vincenzo Bianchi," offered the diminutive man as he extended his hand for a handshake. "Pleasure to meet you."

"I'm Marvin, Marvin Cohen," the tech enthusiast said in a whisper. "Maybe you're overthinking all of this. Perhaps it's entertainment to pass the time until all the stragglers arrive."

"That's a possibility," I acknowledged. Yet, my reservations remained, as I couldn't shake the feeling that there was more to these tests than met the eye.

With a sly grin, Vincenzo handed me my watch, confessing, "One of my hobbies: picking pockets and performing magic tricks."

"While I'm not sure how that could benefit us right now, it's good to know," I responded, albeit with a hint of irritation.

I bypassed a cluster of indoor carnival rides, such as the tilt-a-whirl and merry-go-round, as their circular motion tended to induce nausea. My gaze wandered over them as I moved forward.

Upon reaching the end of the building, I encountered a vast lecture hall with grand double doors leading into it. The layout mirrored a college lecture room, with rows of tiered student desks descending toward a central open area where a teacher might typically deliver their lecture. I wasn't the first to arrive, as others had already taken their seats inside. Some of my fellow candidates were still en route from various stations, loitering by the hall's entrance in hopes of securing a seat once they arrived. Conversations buzzed around me, filling the air with anticipation.

Peering into the lecture hall, I noticed an examination paper on each desk, face down. Printed on the back was a clear directive: "Do not turn over until instructed."

As did many others, I waited outside the room while latecomers trickled in. The clock indicated that it was nearly six o'clock. Observing the situation closely, I realized that six o'clock might be a deadline. Consequently, I ventured into the room but refrained from occupying a seat. Some of my newfound acquaintances soon entered and selected seats toward the rear of the hall, a practice that was in line with most attendees. I continued to assess the situation, contemplating its nuances.

Walking down the center aisle, I halted one-third of the way forward and paused. Suddenly, everything became clear.

Swiftly pivoting, I made my way back through the stream of late arrivals pouring into the room. My companions, intrigued by my abrupt departure, followed me outside. We stood there, watching the final candidates rushing in just before the doors were closed by uniformed guards who had materialized from behind partitions. We were the sole group left outside, accompanied by the guards stationed at each entrance. As we awaited the unfolding events, a palpable sense of anticipation filled the air.

Gradually, a hushed silence descended within the hall, punctuated by faint voices followed by more subdued murmurs. Vincenzo peered out of a side window and beckoned us over.

"Come take a look at this," he urged.

We crowded around the window, gazing at the scene outside. We witnessed disheartened individuals streaming from the hall's side exits, herded like a flock of defeated sheep onto awaiting buses. The sight confirmed my earlier speculation, but I remained uncertain. The others wore expressions of puzzlement, mirroring my uncertainty.

Once the last remnants of the hall's occupants were ushered onto buses and departed, the guards gestured for us to follow them. They escorted us to a small conference room, where we were joined by a distinguished figure—a gray-haired yet remarkably fit man donned in a dark gray suit, a striking red tie, and an American flag lapel pin.

"My name is Darien Dunwoody, Deputy Director of the CIA," he introduced himself. "Mr. Rhodes, I'm pleased to inform you that you've successfully navigated our selection maze."

Initially flattered, I inquired, "What about these others?"

"That decision lies with you," Dunwoody replied.

Perplexed, I sought clarification. "What do you mean?"

"If you choose them to be part of your team, then they, too, will be deemed to have passed," he elaborated. "You are under no obligation to select any of them. Those you decline will be dismissed, and replacements will be provided later. You shall bear responsibility for those you choose."

I surveyed the motley assembly, the tension palpable in the air. My initial instincts inclined me to keep only Abigail, perhaps Jim Smith. However, as I contemplated their diverse skills and strengths, I saw value in an eclectic team that could offer a balanced blend of abilities.

"I'll retain them all," I declared, met with a chorus of enthusiastic "yeahs" and celebratory fist pumps.

Dunwoody delivered a parting statement: "Your selection, as well as theirs, remains contingent on your collective success in the six-week training regimen awaiting you in the weeks ahead. Return to your homes; you will receive directions and instructions on when and where to convene at the training facility called 'The Farm.' Congratulations on your achievements thus far."

As we filed out, boarding the last remaining bus waiting to transport the seven of us back to the parking lot, curiosity ran high among our group. Abigail finally broke the ice.

"We followed you out of the testing hall because you were the first to lead, jumping into the water," she began. "But I think I speak for all of us when I ask, 'How did you know to leave the test room?'"

"It was a hunch," I admitted. "The paper on the desk read, 'Do not turn over until instructed.' It was just a single piece of paper with one large word visible through it, though I couldn't discern the word itself. But logically, the other side could only say either 'passed' or 'failed.' I figured they were attempting to eliminate most candidates, so the paper had to say 'failed.'"

"That's quite a gamble," Vincenzo remarked.

"Sometimes, you have to play the odds as they lean," I responded, with the group nodding in agreement.

We dispersed to our respective homes, awaiting further instructions for our impending training. A week later, an official letter arrived, directing me to report to The Farm at nine o'clock on the first of the month. I anticipated that more formidable challenges awaited us as part of the CIA's entrance process. Moreover, I was determined to uncover any information the CIA might possess regarding my parents' mysterious disappearance and the enigma surrounding the Rumpled Man shooting. My attempts to contact my sister remained fruitless, even after reaching my brother, who professed ignorance of her whereabouts.

CHAPTER 5 LANGLEY VA

Crystal Johnson strode into Dascia Doolittle's office, situated on the third floor of the formidable CIA headquarters. Assigned by Dunwoody, she had been designated as the astute instructor for Jake's team.

Dascia, a mid-thirties woman of Mexican descent with dark hair and dark eyes, was seated behind her desk, a monolithic gray metal structure. Crystal entered and settled into the austere gray metal chair positioned before her. Dascia's appearance was such that she could effortlessly pass for a Russian, a Spaniard, an Italian, an Israeli, or a Czech. With six years of field experience, stationed in Bulgaria and a brief stint in Italy, she had been summoned to headquarters to impart her wisdom to fresh recruits preparing for field assignments. Her ability to infiltrate chauvinistic post-communist government bureaucracies was well-known, but her "politically attuned" colleagues considered her idealistic, a trait that didn't sit well with the field agent "handlers" who received her reports. In the field, where rule-bending was often essential, Dascia was perceived as one who would never bend the rules. However, that perception needed to be more accurate.

Dascia looked up, her eyebrows rising. "Well, to what do I owe the honor of your visit?" she inquired.

"Do you recall the predicament I extricated you from in Madrid six years ago?" Crystal inquired, her gaze piercing Dascia.

"How could I forget? Involving a certain Marcos' heir and a wild weekend that spiraled out of control. It was uncharacteristic of me to lose control while on the job, especially with someone I was supposed to be surveilling."

"I suppose you were surveilling him in a manner of speaking," Crystal retorted with a smirk. "I never asked you to repay that favor."

"Until now?"

"I hear you'll be training a new team of recruits soon."

"Affirmative. How did you find out?"

"You know how well-connected I am."

"Well?" Dascia inquired. "What do you require of me?"

"I want you to ensure that the team leader, Jake Rhodes, fails."

Dascia stood and began pacing. "And why, pray tell, would you want me to do that?"

Let's say I believe he poses a security risk, and we'll leave it at that.

"I'm not certain I can do that," Dascia said, her voice hesitant. "It's not as simple as it sounds."

"You've received extensive sabotage training," Crystal stated. "I'm confident you can devise a solution. For instance, you could administer a unique test to him, including questions on material not covered in class, or conveniently misplace one of his tests, awarding him a zero. Use your imagination."

"I didn't mean I wouldn't know how to do it. I meant I'm not sure I can resort to such deceit."

"I understand your meaning," Crystal replied. "Allow me to clarify mine. You ensure his failure, or I will unearth a long-forgotten file on my desk containing a report by Jackson Alton that details your affair with the individual you were surveilling."

"Geoffrey Alton was killed last year," Dascia murmured.

"Exactly."

Dascia paced back and forth within her cramped office. "Would you truly do this to me? I thought we were friends."

"Oh, we are," Crystal assured her. "After all, what are friends for, if not to assist each other in times of need? And I am in need."

"I will contemplate it."

"You'd best deliberate swiftly and earnestly, my dear. I will be closely monitoring the situation as graduation day approaches."

"And you're perfectly at ease with blackmailing me?"

"Well, let's just say I am doing what I deem necessary and fitting for all parties involved." With those final words, Crystal rose, turned on her heel, and departed, offering no further comments or glances.

Dascia sank heavily into her chair. Training was set to commence the next day, leaving her with little time to devise a strategy.

CHAPTER 6 RURAL VIRGINIA

Our training commenced in early June at the CIA's secluded training facility, nestled in the rural expanse of damp, cool Virginia known as The Farm. Describing this place in detail is outside my purview, but it boasts a range of classroom facilities and extensive areas dedicated to physical training. Typically, basic operations training at this facility spanned a year, depending on specialization. However, our course would be dramatically condensed to just four months, and I had a sneaking suspicion that it would feel like a twelve-month ordeal by the end.

My team awaited me in the reception area upon my arrival. The Agency had provided me with files on each team member to peruse before my appearance, and I had diligently studied each one. Nonetheless, acquainting oneself with someone solely through a dossier has its limitations. I had not yet forged the level of trust required for assignments, let alone entrusting them with my life. I found some solace in my connection with Abigail and Jim, thanks to our shared experiences with donkeys. However, I realized that more time and the right kinds of new adventures would be necessary before extending my trust to all of them if that were ever to happen. Gradually, I understood that, in the espionage business, treachery could lurk at every corner.

My team stood apart from the other trainees, not only in distance but also in appearance. Compared to the

Ivy League look of the others, we were a highly eclectic crew. We had an ex-farmer clad in plaid, an artist adorned with various body decorations and blessed with a photographic memory, a crafty New York Italian street magician, a Techno-nerd with a penchant for stamp collecting, a sports enthusiast who had served as a defensive end for the Iowa Hawkeyes, and Abigail, whose background indicated she had been an Army Ranger and had declined an offer to be the first woman admitted into Army Special Forces training.

While the Ivy League types were dispatched to a classroom to refine their accounting and lawyer skills, Dascia Doolittle, our trainer, arrived with a different agenda. She was a decade older than us but still possessed an undeniable allure. Her arms were sinewy, and her jet-black hair contrasted beautifully with her ice-blue eyes. She exuded a confidence that only experience could bestow.

"Now that you know who I am, let's commence your training," she declared. "Follow me."

Internally, I chuckled, as we knew nothing about her besides her name. As we trailed behind her through a corridor, out into the open space behind the reception building, and down a path leading to a secluded area about half a mile from our initial arrival point, I found myself walking beside Marvin Planck, our nerdiest team member. I couldn't resist asking, "So, what's the deal with your stamp collection?"

Jim, our former farmer, overheard and said, "A stamp collector? Do you still play with Lincoln Logs, too?"

Marvin responded, "You can do many creative things with Lincoln Logs and collecting stamps. Do you collect anything?"

"Not a chance unless you count tractors and cows."

"Many stamps can fetch substantial sums, especially those in the lower Scott numbers if they're mint and perfectly centered, like those in the 130s," Jenny interjected.

"Are you a philatelist?" Marvin inquired.

"Nope," Jenny replied. "I collect an endless stream of memories. That's sufficient for me."

Banter was exchanged among the other team members as well. Dascia's authoritative voice cut through the playful chatter, "Enough of that! Jake, it would be best if you took charge of your team. Cut down on the banter."

"Yes, Lieutenant Doolittle," I responded with military precision.

"And don't call me ma'am. Refer to me as Lieutenant Doolittle."

"Roger that," I acknowledged, adhering to her directive.

The training area resembled my time in Army boot camp, complete with several barracks, a modest mess hall, an obstacle course, a firing range, and several classroom buildings.

Each phase of our training had us on the edge, metaphorically speaking, with the looming possibility of failing at the end of each stage. Our training was divided into three phases. The first phase was intensely physical, involving rigorous exercise routines and daily runs through the obstacle course. We also received basic weapons and self-defense training. Each of us was equipped with a custom version of the Smith-Wesson Walther PK380, slightly smaller than the Walther PK 40 famously wielded by James Bond. These compact yet potent handguns boasted accuracy up to approximately 50 yards for the average agent. Additionally, we were issued small "silencers," with the caveat that they merely muffled the sound but did not eliminate it.

Dascia cautioned us about the risk of carrying a silenced pistol, emphasizing that it could expose us as agents. We also received preliminary training in various "specialty" weapons, which we were instructed not to discuss but were unlikely to employ. We all effortlessly passed the firearms training, with Abigail and I achieving the titles of Markswoman and Marksman.

We developed a deep admiration and fondness for Dascia as the training progressed. She proved deceptively intelligent and remarkably fit, leading us through every exercise with impressive vigor. I was pleasantly surprised by the ability of Marvin, our techno-nerd, Jenny, the artist, and Vincenzo, our Italian magician, to keep up. Surprisingly, the two individuals who encountered difficulties but met the minimum requirements were Jim, the farmer, and Max, the football player. Despite their muscular builds, their endurance had waned due to their size and lack of conditioning. Armed with her recent Army training, Abigail consistently ranked at the top of the class, consistently outperforming me in every test. Her competitiveness occasionally rubbed me the wrong way, but overall, we progressed well. Nevertheless, Dascia remained tight-lipped about how she was evaluating our performance.

The second phase of our training focused on communications security, specifically coded message transmission. Jerome Wallace, another trainer, took charge of this subject. Our primary tool was a set of numbered paper pads, each featuring a unique code key at the top of every page. To send a coded message, the sender would utilize the codes from one of the pages, transmitting both the message and the corresponding page number. The recipient would then use a matching pad to decode the message using the key provided. This method ensured that eavesdroppers could not decipher the message without access to the matching page.

Dascia dismissed most secret message training, including computer-based methods, as impractical for undercover agents, as agents in urgent situations rarely had access to a compatible keypad or computer. She recommended using the telephone and speaking cryptically as the most pragmatic approach. Consequently, there were no tests for us to pass in this phase.

The third and most challenging phase of our training delved into the most clandestine aspects of our job. We received instruction on various electronic devices, with Marvin emerging as the standout in electronics due to his prior experience in repairing electronic devices. We also learned about interrogation techniques, torture methods and even delved into the bureaucratic paperwork of the "Company." Every organization has its forms, and everyone on our team handled this training adeptly. I saw no reason why we all wouldn't graduate.

While we immersed ourselves in our training, an undercurrent of conspiracy simmered beneath the surface of the "Company." Little did we know that if we completed our training, we might be on a collision course with that discord.

CHAPTER 7 LANGLEY VA

Unbeknownst to Randall Rogers, the Director of the CIA, he sat behind his sleek glass-top desk in the most prominent corner office atop the CIA headquarters in Langley, Virginia. Rogers had held the post of Head of the CIA for a decade, a man in his mid-fifties with another ten years before retirement loomed on his horizon. His hair had long retreated into a monk-like shape, his physique had succumbed to his gradual descent into fitness negligence, and the shadows under his eyes bore witness to his weariness. Already, he yearned for the day when he could begin to forget all that he had come to know.

His management style blended aloofness with a hint of mild arrogance, tinged with a touch of professorial ineptitude. This disposition often isolated him from the knowledge of critical activities transpiring below his department, matters of which he should have been well informed. His detachment stemmed from the need to become more immersed in day-to-day affairs or, at the very least, more receptive to the counsel of those under his command.

"Bea, get Dunwoody," he called out to his long-serving administrative assistant stationed at her desk just outside his door.

"He's already here, waiting for you with Crystal Johnson," she replied from the outer office as Darien Dunwoody and Crystal Johnson entered. Dunwoody could have effortlessly passed as a Nazi SS Officer during World War II. Tall, trim, and moderately muscular, he possessed an angular face, a full head of wavy blond hair, and an unyielding demeanor. After commencing his career as a field agent merely a decade ago, he had ascended the ranks swiftly, now serving as Deputy Director under Rogers. Dunwoody was a polyglot, fluently conversant in half a dozen languages, each delivered with the appropriate accent. If he exercised patience and avoided missteps, he stood as a leading contender to succeed Rogers upon the latter's retirement in another ten years. However, Rogers harbored reservations about Dunwoody's capacity for patience and half-expected him to seize a lucrative defense industry executive position at any moment. What Rogers did not realize was that Dunwoody possessed a far greater cunning than he had imagined, with plans to take over well before Rogers's retirement.

"What do you know about this Gerald Wilson case?" Rogers inquired.

"We're still investigating," Dunwoody responded. "Crystal, enlighten the Director with our current findings."

"Well, I'm uncertain if this constitutes good or bad news," she began. "The Secret Service delivered the body of one Gerald Wilson to us, along with a briefcase that implicates him in espionage."

"Espionage? For whom? I've never heard of him."

"The details remain murky," she explained. "Based on the briefcase's contents, it appears Wilson was a foreign agent operating within the U.S. on behalf of the SVR."

"It seems too conspicuous for the Russians, almost too convenient."

"The Secret Service initiated this after intercepting intelligence and monitoring a known Soviet operative, hoping he would lead them to an unidentified SVR spy," she continued. "It was this operative who handed the briefcase to Wilson."

"The Secret Service? Not our people? How did this unfold?"

"Both the operative and Wilson were shot and killed on the spot. It occurred at a black-tie charity gala at the Gaylord, effectively disrupting their fundraising efforts. We've managed to suppress news coverage of the incident so far. Our agents were briefed about the operation but did not participate."

"Who fired the shots?"

"The Secret Service did not discharge their weapons," she clarified. "An unknown assailant shot both victims from a nearby stairwell. According to the agents present, the assailant was a sharpshooter."

"A room filled with Secret Service agents couldn't prevent the shooter from escaping after committing the double murder?"

"It appears not," she conceded. "The shooter fired shots above the heads of the crowd, exploiting the ensuing chaos to make a clean getaway."

"There must be more to this. Keep me informed as we gather additional details. Also, discreetly probe for information about the shooter—Interpol, MI5, and even the SVR. See if anyone provides any insights."

"Of course, Director," she responded loud enough for him to hear as she departed, with Dunwoody following.

Outside the Director's office, Dunwoody whispered to Crystal, "Well done." However, Crystal didn't catch his praise as her thoughts revolved around Dascia and whether she was following her instructions. Dascia aimed to ensure her brother remained untangled in their weaving web.

Returning to her office down the hall, Crystal reached for the telephone. Her workspace epitomized an organized work area, with papers meticulously arranged in matching mahogany in-and-out boxes and books neatly lined on the shelves, all standing erect between bookends. Not a single photograph or plant adorned her space to provide personalization.

"This is Crystal. Why haven't you acted yet?" she inquired over the phone.

"Too many witnesses have observed his performance during core training," Dascia responded. "It would raise too many questions. Rest assured; I will have him to myself during their trial assignment. I'll address it when I conduct their assessment. It's a real shame, though, if I may say so. He genuinely possesses the potential to be an excellent agent. He's a natural leader."

"Let's not dwell on that; just follow our plan," Crystal instructed.

She heard Dascia mutter as she hung up, "I don't recall this being a discussion."

Crystal allowed herself a small smile as she left her office to initiate the process of gathering information about the shooter. Still, her thoughts lingered on Jake as she remained anxious that Dascia might not fulfill her request.

CHAPTER 8 WASHINGTON DC

We completed our training, but none of us had yet heard if we had graduated. Back at my apartment in DC, the first thing I did was call my sister. Like last time, no answer. I decided to try again that evening and if there was no answer I would go over to her house in the morning and find the underlying cause of what was going on with her.

She still didn't answer her phone that evening; so, the next morning I drove to her house. This time, there were no newspapers on the front porch. When I knocked, like last time, no one came to the door. I looked in the windows and could see that the house was quiet and looked as undisturbed as it was last time, so I decided not to bother letting myself in. I could see unread newspapers spread out on the dining table, so someone had to have taken them in. Given it was 9:00 AM, I reckoned she was at work or hopefully her school administrator would know something, so I headed there. I wasn't sure how worried I should be.

At her school, I went to the office where, I hoped, they would summon my sister from her classroom. The office administrator told me that she was on vacation and would be back in two weeks. I found that odd. Even though a couple of months had passed, I thought she might have called me if she was planning a big trip. I left a message with the school's administrative office to have Crystal call me and let them know I would return in two weeks. I went back to my apartment to wait to learn if we all passed our training.

Two days later, I received a certified letter. I paced back and forth a few times holding the unopened letter in my hands. Eventually, my hopes overtook my fear of rejection, and I tore it open. The letter informed me that I had passed and was to report the following Monday for orientation and first assignment. It also said that I was not to reveal to anyone the letter's contents. I was delighted but also concerned -- it made no mention of my team. Oddly, the letter directed me to enter CIA headquarters through the loading dock door in the rear of the facility. That didn't sound designed to impress a new recruit. I worried about my team and wondered why the Company was planning such a low-profile entrance for our first day. I barely slept between getting the letter and Monday morning.

CHAPTER 9 LANGLEY VA

On Monday morning, precisely at 9:00 AM, I entered through the designated loading dock door. Inside, the rest of my team and our trainer, Lieutenant Dascia Doolittle, awaited me in a wide-open area with a concrete floor reminiscent of a typical warehouse.

Dascia addressed us, saying, "I apologize for this discreet entrance, but we aim to maintain a low profile, especially concerning other agents. From this day forward, safeguarding your identities is of utmost importance."

A question crossed my mind: "Why all this secrecy? Are there people within the CIA we can't trust?"

Dascia continued, "The more unassuming you appear in your looks and the less conspicuous you are in your behavior, the more successful you will be in this role."

Abigail added, "You mean the longer we'll survive."

Dascia nodded and went on, "That too. However, let me clarify your status. You won't be secure in your positions until you complete your first assignment. Starting today, we'll treat you like fully-fledged agents, but your permanent status depends on your performance during this initial mission. Consider yourselves on probation, so pay close attention."

Dascia gave me "the look" and led us down a hallway into a small conference room, where our credentials and official Walther handguns had been arranged on a table. She instructed us to schedule several hours of training at a local shooting range of our choice to become familiar with the Walther. This training would help us adapt to the long trigger pull, designed to prevent accidental discharges when drawing the weapon.

Our credentials consisted of a simple replacement for our state driver's licenses, featuring a code "C" on the back, where the organ donor and eyeglasses information typically goes. I assumed the "C" could prove our affiliation with the agency if another government agent ever confronted us. The licenses had yet to be laminated, and Dascia asked us to sign our photographs, matching the name on the license. As I examined my driver's license more closely, I noticed that the name on it was different from my own. A glance at my teammates' licenses revealed that the same was true for all of us. Suddenly, we were individuals with entirely new identities, raising my curiosity about our ability to adopt these different personas convincingly.

Dascia also distributed new passports bearing our new names for us to sign. We received two passports each: one American and another from a different country, with English as the primary language in the second. My new passport identified me as Australian, while Abigail's indicated Canadian nationality. Other team members received similar variations. I surmised that the second passport was intended for use in situations where being a U.S. citizen would be less advantageous. Dascia then provided us with yet another set of entirely different documentation, endowing us with two distinct identities, neither of which matched our actual selves. My concern grew over how we would discreetly carry this stack of documents without it drawing attention or becoming mixed up. We followed Dascia's instructions and signed each set as directed. She collected them, walked to the door, and called for someone to retrieve them for final processing. Dascia then instructed us to raise our right hand and repeat after her, during which we recited an oath of allegiance to the agency and country using our real names. The oath officially inducted us as employees of the U.S. Government, affording us some legal protection for our actions in the line of duty.

After being sworn in, we gathered around the table, ready to receive our first mission briefing. Just as Lieutenant Dascia Doolittle was about to start, a grey-haired man with strikingly bright blue eyes briefly poked his head into the room, glanced at each of us without introducing himself, and hastily excused himself as if he had walked into the wrong room. Anonymity, I thought, had just flown out the window.

Dascia continued, undeterred, "For your inaugural assignment, I'll oversee your investigation of a large company here in DC that we suspect has been infiltrated by a foreign industrial spy. It's a significant technology firm handling government military contracts, and it's been hemorrhaging classified information to foreign competitors. The only plausible explanation is an insider spy. This agent is selling sensitive data to the Chinese, but we can't jump to conclusions about their nationality. We have no information on the spy's characteristics; we only know that the company loses secrets to China weekly. Your mission involves assuming new identities and taking on various roles within the company to blend in."

Just as Dascia was about to delve into more details, another older gentleman entered the room. Dascia introduced him, saying, "This is Darien Dunwoody, the Assistant Director of the CIA and my superior, making him your boss as well."

In response, we offered greetings in various forms.

Dunwoody said, "I wanted to drop by and welcome you to the agency. My office door is always open, so if you ever need assistance from me or my team, don't hesitate to visit."

Dascia's reaction didn't escape my notice – a subtle expression that hinted at skepticism. I made a mental note to inquire about it later. Dunwoody quietly exited the room, leaving me with an uncomfortable feeling about him – too smooth, too detached.

With Dunwoody's departure, Dascia continued, distributing the remainder of our new identities, issuing credit cards with our assumed names, and asking us to sign them on the back. She also assigned each of us fictitious roles for the upcoming investigation. She then passed around a basket, instructing us to deposit our existing identification, including everything in our wallets or purses that could reveal our true identities. Dascia would hold onto these items until after the assignment to eliminate any chances of mistakes. She emphasized the importance of practicing our new names until they became second nature and encouraged us to create comprehensive backstories for our personas, covering aspects such as our upbringing, job history, and why our accents didn't match our identities. We were to base these backstories on familiar facts and avoid references that could be traced back to us.

At this point, a young lady returned with our new licenses, now laminated, and our passports, bearing stamps and embossments.

Dascia then explained the roles assigned to us, designed to ensure we were distributed across the company without any apparent association. The assignments were as follows:

I was to be a copier repairman.

Jim would take on the role of a janitor.

Abigail would work as a new admin in the legal department.

Jenny was designated as a new graphic artist.

Vincenzo assumed the position of a new sales representative.

Max, incongruously, was tasked with being a caterer.

Marvin, a programmer by trade, would take that role within the company.

The assigned roles left me with some questions, but I anticipated we would refine our plan among ourselves.

Dascia then informed us of our starting point: The Taylor Company headquarters near 14th Street Northwest at Riggs St. We were to arrive punctually at 9:00 AM on Wednesday. Dascia distributed a sheet detailing our respective assignments within the company, specifying that the company's executives were aware of our arrival only at the highest level and within HR. For those assigned to departments, the department heads would be informed that we were new hires. Dascia emphasized our role: discreetly monitoring for suspicious activities, such as unauthorized access to file drawers, going through trash bins, or concealing documents. She cautioned against drawing attention and recommended using mirrors, window reflections, or discreet glances to observe without being overt. We were not to confront any potential suspects independently but to alert Dascia, who would be stationed at the lobby entrance guard's desk via phone at extension 8282 or by visiting the lobby in case of phone unavailability.

Although Dascia was a stern trainer, we had all developed a fondness for her. Nevertheless, the level of preparation provided to our new team was lacking. I was unwilling to leave anything to chance, regarding my limited knowledge of copier repair. While I knew how to open copier doors and follow the instructions inside, I was clueless beyond that, even when operating the controls. I felt exposed with such basic training but chose to withhold my concerns for the time being, waiting for the right moment to address them.

As Dascia concluded, she shared our schedule, granting us a day off to practice with our Walthers before our rendezvous Wednesday morning at The Taylor Company.

With Dascia's departure, I initiated a discussion with the team, proposing, "I think we should convene to plan this assignment in more detail than what we've been provided. What do you all think?"

Abigail agreed, stating, "Dascia has been excellent, but every trainer has their limits, and we'll need to take charge eventually." The consensus was evident among the group.

"Let's meet tomorrow at 8 AM at the McDonald's on Old Dominion Drive," I suggested. "We have just one day to strategize and fulfill our prescribed training."

Unbeknownst to us, as we plotted the intricacies of our upcoming mission, the far-reaching arms of a conspiratorial storm were silently extending across the world, akin to the most colossal hurricane humanity had ever encountered.

CHAPTER 10 MOSCOW

On the far side of the world, in Moscow, Harold Harper, an unassuming Englishman, occupied a solitary spot at a quaint sidewalk cafe in a middle-class neighborhood. It was an unusually mild day in March, and he sat in leisure, unaware of the pivotal role he was about to play in a global conspiracy. Harper calmly sipped a diminutive cup of robust, black coffee while perusing the previous day's edition of the London Times. He was of middle age, slightly overweight, and had a soft, almost cushion-like appearance, accentuated by his neatly combed salt-and-pepper hair—a familiar look for many Britons that often concealed an unexpectedly resilient interior. His attention was diverted when an inconspicuous, dark-haired Spanish woman discreetly placed a manila envelope on the empty chair across from him. As he approached retirement in a year and a half and currently lacking an assignment, he relished this rare opportunity for relaxation. Yet, in espionage, unwinding could be a perilous mistake, particularly in Russia.

Unbeknownst to Harper, two burly men in suits promptly approached as the woman vanished from the cafe's confined sidewalk seating area. The larger of the two men reached Harper's table first and boomed, "Mr. Harper, come with us." His name was Egor Federov, but he saw no need for introductions. His imposing stature, military-style haircut, and taut biceps visible beneath his jacket sleeves provided ample credentials.

Harper glanced up, surprised and bewildered at the unexpected attention, and inquired with a composed demeanor, "How do you know my name?"

"We've been observing you for some time," stated the smaller man, failing to offer his name. He, too, was muscular and sported an identical haircut, but had a leaner build. Eugeny Titov attempted to emulate Federov, an idol in his eyes.

"At what am I red-handed, as you claim?" Harper inquired calmly.

"Accepting this parcel from a known American spy," the hulking man declared, brandishing the envelope he had retrieved from the chair. The few remaining cafe patrons shifted uncomfortably in their seats as if fearing they might be next. A young couple quickly abandoned their chairs and scurried away.

"I have no idea what you're talking about," Harper responded. "I don't know where that came from; I didn't know it was there, and I certainly don't know what it contains. Your charade is beginning to resemble a clumsy setup."

"We'll see about that," the diminutive man said, seizing Harper's elbow and prompting him to stand. Harper didn't offer much resistance but didn't comply willingly either.

The two men swiftly ushered Harper down the street and into an inconspicuous, unmarked white van that immediately sped away.

As they vanished around the corner, the elegantly attired Spanish woman returned to Harper's table, sat, and leisurely perused his newspaper. Meanwhile, the cafe owner collected the used dishes.

"I'll have a cup of coffee if you don't mind," she requested in a husky voice. "Charge it to the previous gentleman's bill." She picked up Harper's newspaper and perused an article titled *"Catholic Church Experiencing Decline in Followers."*

CHAPTER 11 WASHINGTON DC

At McDonald's the following morning, we initiated our independent planning session. We needed to solidify our team dynamics and prepare for potential contingencies our trainer might have covered more thoroughly.

Our discussion encompassed various aspects, including our conduct upon arrival at the target location and strategies to streamline our operation. We contemplated using profiling, not in terms of physical appearance, as a spy could take any form but rather focusing on behaviors indicative of an industrial spy. For instance, we considered that such a spy might arrive early or stay late, attempt to acquire another person's computer password or access card, or even gain access to locked rooms. We discussed the likelihood that the spy would blend in seamlessly with others, exhibiting no distinct accent or noticeable traits, as spies aim to remain inconspicuous and avoid drawing attention to themselves. We also conjectured that our spy would be intelligent and highly skilled in concealing their identity, including a willingness to deny wrongdoing if confronted to protect their organization. Furthermore, we hypothesized that the spy's target might include military-related information or intellectual property, such as new patent applications, which led us to focus on the Product Development and Legal departments.

We deliberated over our roles and made a couple of swaps. Max had experience as a copier repairman, and Jim knew about food preparation, so I exchanged my role for that of a janitor, and Jim assumed the role of a caterer. Max even had his old copier repair uniform, and I had some clothes from my past that suited a janitor's appearance. Abigail mentioned that she had a Security Guard uniform from a previous job. Our discussion prompted us to develop a secondary set of roles, one for each of us, ready for deployment if needed after business hours. We also considered refining these secondary roles for future use whenever we needed to maintain a low profile. We agreed to work late into the evening if we didn't identify the suspect during the day and prepared to transition into janitorial staff, except for Abigail, who would remain in her role as a watchwoman.

Lastly, we discussed the floors on which we would begin our assignments and our communication methods, particularly for those of us moving between floors. We devised a set of hand signals akin to those used by a third base coach in baseball: touching our nose indicated a suspect, scratching an ear signified no leads yet, and placing both hands on our face signaled the need to gather behind the building near the dumpsters. To request a team member to relocate to a different floor, we devised a discreet method of dropping a piece of paper with a number. The other agent would pick it up, glance at it briefly, and casually discard it in a trash can to avoid arousing suspicion. I reiterated that our primary objective was to identify the person and not apprehend them; Dascia would handle the arrest once we provided her with the target's identity. With our plans in place, we departed in different directions to visit local gun ranges for additional training with our Walthers. We were set to reconvene at the target office building the following morning, ready to embrace the life of a CIA agent.

We infiltrated the business premises in the early hours of the following day, operating under our newly assumed identities. The building's interior boasted gleaming marble floors and polished stainless-steel elevator doors. Since Wednesday was the typical day for new hires, the sudden influx of fresh faces went unnoticed, particularly given the company's rapid growth and occupation of seven floors in the spacious high-rise office building. We strategically dispersed to various floors based on our assigned roles.

Max immediately put his expertise to use. Leveraging his knowledge of copiers, he accessed each machine's internal memory to retrieve images of the last items copied. This early morning endeavor aimed to capture any evidence of individuals who had arrived early or stayed late the previous night for covert copying. Max, using personnel records and potential target products, narrowed down the possible location of our spy to two floors, the tenth and the twelfth. Subsequently, we commenced surveillance on the copiers situated on these floors.

It was a long day of maintaining our nondescript personas, a more challenging task than one might imagine. Throughout the day, we did not observe anyone exhibiting suspicious behavior. Therefore, once the office had closed for the day, we convened at the rear of the building to transition into our secondary roles as watchmen and cleaning staff. We were banking on office workers not paying attention to those responsible for tidying up their workplace.

To ensure comprehensive coverage, we stationed Marvin and Jenny at both the front and rear exits in case the spy attempted to escape. We also communicated with Dascia to confirm her presence at her designated post.

At eight o'clock that evening, while some of us diligently carried out our cleaning duties on the tenth floor, a young man arrived at one of the photocopiers, clutching an armful of files. I edged closer, pretending to be engrossed in emptying a nearby trash can. I sensed his gaze on me but continued my work, feigning indifference. As expected, when I did not react to his presence, he resumed his activities. From the corner of my eye, I saw a document cover showing the words "Security Classification: Secret." It was a strong indicator that this individual was our spy. I moved away and subtly touched my nose to signal Jim. Jim discreetly maneuvered his cleaning cart toward the elevator lobby, eventually entering an elevator. Upon reaching the lobby level, he swiftly informed Dascia, who promptly ascended the elevator with Jim and her team of security guards. Upon disembarking on the tenth floor, they immediately spotted the young spy, and he noticed them too. Realizing he was cornered, he abandoned the copier and made a quick dash toward his office down the corridor. Unfortunately for him, he didn't get far. The security guards apprehended him swiftly and verified his identity as the culprit.

CHAPTER 12 WASHINGTON DC

Dascia had just begun addressing us when Rebecca Carter, the Assistant Director, entered from outside. She commanded a stern presence as Dascia's superior and the liaison between Dascia and Dunwoody. Tall and impeccably dressed in a standard corporate suit, she exuded an aura of professionalism. In her mid-forties, Carter appeared entirely business-focused. Stepping forward to address our diverse group, she didn't mince words.

"This was meant to be a two to three-day exercise, you lot," she remarked, a hint of exasperation in her voice. "Yet, you managed to uncover the spy in a single day – a long day, but one day, nonetheless. I should give you a hard time for messing up the schedule, but I must concede – well done."

We exchanged smiles and glances, our satisfaction palpable.

"However," Carter continued, "I have some unfortunate news. The 'spy' was one of our agents. This assignment was a trial exercise designed to evaluate your teamwork. Since you performed exceptionally well, your next assignment will be real. This task was relatively low-risk, but future assignments may become progressively more perilous. I strongly encourage you to maintain your vigilance. We may send people to shadow you, or others might. Vigilance is a habit developed through practice, even in your sleep."

"Did Dascia know this was just a training exercise?" I inquired.

"No," Carter replied.

"I suppose I was also being evaluated," Dascia chimed in. "That's frustrating."

"She is still responsible for assessing your performance on this assignment," Carter clarified. "Based on her evaluations, we will determine whether you have completed your probationary period. Nothing is guaranteed."

With that, Carter dismissed us and left the premises while we lingered to review what had worked and what hadn't. Our planning was effective, particularly in aligning our roles with our personal experiences. However, we chided ourselves for not anticipating the need to work a second shift. If we had, we could have provided more convincing disguises to support our second round of interaction with the same people. We agreed to diversify our disguises and become proficient in our secondary identities. I regretted not recognizing that the "spy" was a setup. In retrospect, leaving the Top-Secret file face-up should have been a giveaway.

As the group disbanded, Dascia was the first to depart, her family awaiting her at home. We had grown attached to her, knowing she would advance in her career while we embarked on new assignments.

However, as soon as Dascia cleared the revolving door, I noticed something amiss out of the corner of my eye. She suddenly collapsed, her fall abrupt and alarming. At first, I assumed she had tripped. Reacting instinctively, I rushed to the door to help her, with the others close behind. But as I reached her, I realized the situation was grave. She lay sprawled headfirst on the unyielding marble steps, completely motionless. Instinctively, I checked for her pulse, but something unusual caught my attention. My hand brushed against a small object, an inch long, adorned with short feathers. It was a dart, like those fired from dart guns – a silent and potentially lethal weapon when coated with poison. My immediate suspicion turned to this possibility. Drawing my pistol, I meticulously scanned the vicinity, examining every nook and cranny from ground level to the rooftops. My colleagues followed suit, dispersing to investigate different exit routes. There was no trace of the assailant, leaving us to conclude that Dascia had been the deliberate target.

"Call headquarters," I instructed urgently. "And have dispatch notify Carter immediately."

"Should I dial 911?" Abigail inquired.

"No," I replied, my gut feeling telling me that the Agency didn't involve local law enforcement in such matters. My reasoning stemmed from the conspicuous absence of CIA-related incidents in local media.

Within minutes, Carter arrived on the scene, her face flushed with concern. "Did anyone call 911?" she asked. My heart leaped into my throat, fearing I had made a mistake.

Abigail quickly interjected, "Not yet. We thought it best to await your guidance before taking any action."

"Excellent decision," Carter affirmed. "We have our own teams to handle situations like this." An ambulance pulled up at that moment.

"Is that one of ours?" I queried.

"Precisely," Carter responded. "You can all depart now before attracting undue attention or compromising your identities. Let's make it appear to be a straightforward slip and fall."

"Have you encountered such scenarios before?" I inquired.

"Meet me at Langley tomorrow morning," she replied, "and I'll brief you on what we know."

I couldn't help but contemplate the gravity of the situation. We had suddenly stumbled upon a complex and perilous predicament. My heart went out to Dascia's family; her demise would remain unexplained, devoid of public acknowledgment. It was a situation I knew all too well, harkening back to the day I learned of my parents' deaths.

Naturally, our team felt a sense of responsibility to address this injustice.

CHAPTER 13 LANGLEY VA

The following morning, our rendezvous took place at headquarters. We arrived at the loading dock door, forming a line as we entered the same conference room where our initial assembly occurred. This time, Darien Dunwoody was waiting for us, flanked by an enigmatic man and an elegant woman from his staff whom he neglected to introduce initially. He began the briefing once we were all present and settled into our seats.

"We possess limited information about Dascia's assailants, but we can confirm that agents from Bucharest were responsible," he declared.

Curiosity gnawed at me, and I couldn't help but ask, "How did we come to this conclusion?"

Dunwoody's eyes scanned the room before he explained, "Our suspicion arose when we were tracking a pair of enigmatic Romanians who entered the country on questionable visas. However, they managed to evade us yesterday, employing a cunning maneuver. They arranged for two similarly dressed locals from Bucharest to traverse a coffee shop just as they did. While one team exited, the other entered. This switch occurred as we changed tracking teams, causing a momentary lapse in our surveillance. We only realized the original agents had concealed themselves in the cafe about an hour after we tracked the substitutes to the Romanian embassy. Surprisingly, both impostors held positions as attaches to the embassy, making them untouchable. Meanwhile, the true agents were free to locate and assassinate Dascia."

Vincenzo inquired, "So, you're suggesting the Romanian government's involvement?"

Dunwoody shook his head, dispelling that notion. "We have compelling reasons to believe otherwise. The perpetrators seem to have infiltrated Romania's diplomatic ranks as a cover, but their embassy roles appear authentic, rendering them immune to interrogation."

"The precision of their replacement team placement suggests inside knowledge," I noted, my skepticism growing. Dunwoody nodded subtly.

Jenny posed an important question, "But why target Dascia?"

"Many ex-KGB agents relocated to Bucharest after the fall of the Iron Curtain," Dunwoody elucidated. "Having been supplanted by a new generation, these 'old school' agents turned to industrial espionage. It offered greater financial rewards and less danger—until now. However, we lack information regarding any connection between Dascia and this rogue group or their motive for targeting her. To our knowledge, she had been exclusively involved in training for the past five years. We have teams actively investigating any potential connections."

A chill ran down my spine, reminiscent of when I learned of my parents' deaths—cold, unfeeling messages and emotionless deliveries. Instinctively, I harbored suspicions about Dunwoody.

"What was the cause of death?" I inquired.

Dunwoody responded, "It appears to be regency-grade Tubocurarine chloride, commonly known as curare—the same poison used on hunting arrows by South American natives. The dart was likely fired from an air pistol."

Jim pressed further, "Shouldn't we pursue the culprits?"

Dunwoody shook his head firmly. "No. We've assigned a more seasoned team to handle this situation."

Abigail interjected with determination, "We want to be the ones to bring Dascia's killers to justice."

Dunwoody's tone remained unwavering. "We aim to keep emotions out of our operations. Your proximity to Dascia might compromise your objectivity and lead to impulsive actions. Furthermore, we seldom engage in direct retaliatory measures."

Unfazed, Abigail persisted, "And I presume you weren't particularly close to her?"

Ignoring her remark, Dunwoody continued, "How this 'problem' will be handled is on a need-to-know basis only. I'm assigning you a new trainer, Jerome Wallace. He's been a fixture within the agency for many years."

Seated at the table's end, Wallace, in his fifties, possessed an overweight frame and receding hairline but compensated with lively eyes and an authentic smile.

"Call me Jerry," Jerome offered.

"Jerome has a somewhat checkered history with the agency, but he'll play by the rules for the next 18 months, as he'll be eligible for retirement then," Dunwoody added.

"Jerry suits me just fine," Jerome quipped. "I won't let impending retirement or veiled pension threats sway me."

Dunwoody corrected him, "That wasn't a veiled threat. Stick to the rulebook for the remaining months if you desire a comfortable retirement. Also, allow me to introduce Cindy Madison, my administrative assistant."

Cindy, a short and buxom blonde, nervously chewed gum, projecting an appearance of naivety. However, her position belied any such impression.

Vincenzo couldn't resist a flirtatious remark, "We were wondering when you'd introduce us to the lovely blonde."

With a giggle, Cindy greeted us, "Hello, everybody."

"Mr. Dunwoody," I interjected, "Allow us to pursue these agents. While it's true we have a personal vendetta, I believe we can maintain our objectivity."

Dunwoody responded firmly, "The answer is no, and emphatically so. Moreover, you lack the necessary information even to begin."

I proposed an alternative, "What if Jake and his team assist from headquarters? We can conduct research and gather information. This way, we may contribute constructively to the investigation."

Dunwoody weighed my suggestion before conceding, "Very well, but solely as a training exercise. I'll adjust your clearances to limited top secret for this purpose. If you uncover anything significant, you'll report it to me immediately. Is that understood?"

"Yes, sir," I affirmed.

Dunwoody concluded, "They're under your purview now," as he exited the room, trailed by Cindy Madison.

As soon as Dunwoody left, Jerry beckoned us closer, ensuring our conversation remained confidential. He returned our genuine identification documents, collected by Dascia earlier, as he began to speak.

"The agency won't take meaningful action regarding Dascia's murder," Jerry declared, his voice filled with certainty. "I've seen it happen too many times to doubt it."

Marvin inquired, "Why not?"

Jerry expounded, "The agency is stretched thin, and they view someone like Dascia as expendable—a remnant of the Cold War they claim to have ended, though it lingers on. Head up to the library on the third floor, and then reconvene here around 4:00 PM with any relevant findings you can unearth—anything that might remotely help. Approach this assignment as a valuable exercise with the right attitude. Meanwhile, I'll check a few leads with my contacts on the floors above."

With that, Jerry left us alone to contemplate our next steps.

"I'm deeply troubled by the agency's indifference to Dascia's murder," I said. "There's more to this than meets the eye. And I can't help but suspect Jerry has his agenda, possibly to prolong our training until his retirement. We might have to take matters into our own hands. Let's head to the library and see what resources we can gather."

CHAPTER 14 LANGLEY VA

While my team and I grappled with the shock of Dascia's death, Crystal found herself alone in Dascia's office, meticulously searching through her desk to uncover any clues that might shed light on the tragedy.

Learning of Dascia's demise had left Crystal deeply distraught. It signified that Jake had completed his training and transitioned into active duty. Her involvement with Dunwoody had reached such a point that she could no longer take any direct actions to safeguard her brother. Her only recourse was to keep a significant distance from Jake at all costs, ensuring that he remained unaware of her affiliation with the CIA and preventing anyone else from discovering their familial connection.

Crystal pulled open the center desk drawer, avoiding the handles and pulling it open with her fingers. To her surprise, after carefully removing the papers within, she pulled the entire drawer from its housing, emptying its remaining contents of pens, paperclips, and assorted office supplies onto the desk's surface. Hidden beneath the drawer was a manila envelope, which Crystal extracted—an ominous file folder. Her shock intensified when she saw her parents' names typed on the folder's tab. Overwhelmed, she settled into Dascia's desk chair and began perusing the contents, discerning from the labeling that they had been removed from the confidential archives in the agency's library.

The file contained two reports, one of which detailed the circumstances surrounding her parents' deaths, labeling them as assassinations by an unidentified foreign entity. It described how they had been fatally shot in the back of the head while seated in the front of a car. This description implied that the car windows must have been down, and they were either taken by surprise or acquainted with their assailant(s). The report was the official narrative.

Within the midst of the second report, nestled between routine official documents, Crystal found a compilation of notes penned by her father to her mother. These notes hinted at an unspecified conspiracy and raised suspicions that Dunwoody might be at its epicenter as far as the CIA was concerned. This revelation posed a grave threat to Crystal's ongoing plans, and she realized that these notes must not become known at this critical juncture. She pondered why Dascia possessed this file—was she attempting to protect Crystal, potentially as a counterbalance to the pressure she had placed on Dascia regarding Jake's performance, or was there another motive at play?

Crystal understood that Dunwoody must not become aware of this file's existence, and she recognized the urgency of restoring it to its rightful place within the agency's library archives. She carefully removed the vital pages from the stapled second report, ensuring no trace of her tampering remained. After restoring the office to its original state and finding no additional clues related to Dascia's assassination, Crystal promptly returned the file to its designated location in the library records. Uncertain of what to do with the extracted pages, she resolved to conceal them meticulously, understanding that they held vital information she might need in the future.

CHAPTER 15 MOSCOW

Several hours later, half a world away in Moscow, Leonid Demodov, the Managing Director of the SVR, found himself seated behind a grand mahogany desk dating back to the Stalin era. He occupied a spacious, high-ceilinged room within the SVR's headquarters building. An overhead fan whirred quietly, casting a gentle breeze. SVR was the abbreviation for Sluzhba Vneshney Razvedki, translating to "Foreign Intelligence Service" in Russian. As the head of the Russian intelligence agency, Demodov oversaw all foreign intelligence operations, akin to the CIA's role in the United States. However, he possessed the authority to delve into domestic affairs whenever it suited his interests, and no one dared to challenge him. Physically, he was an imposing figure with robust forearms, a barrel chest, and a personality to match. He assumed control of the SVR as the Cold War ended, guiding his organization through the transformation following the collapse of the Soviet Union.

The SVR collaborated closely with the Russian Main Intelligence Directorate, known as the GRU, the overarching intelligence agency of the Russian military. The GRU was rumored to have deployed six times more spies in foreign countries than the SVR since the Cold War's conclusion. Nonetheless, the SVR wielded more significant influence over the country's president than the GRU, often operating discreetly behind the scenes, particularly in shaping Russian foreign policy. Situated discreetly in the Yasenevo District of Moscow, the SVR's office building maintained a low profile, much like the CIA's facility in Langley, Virginia.

Demodov was engrossed in reading intelligence reports when his administrative assistant knocked on his open office door and entered, her graceful stride causing her skirt to sway enticingly. She was an attractive young blonde with vivid red lipstick and a form-fitting sweater, clearly catching her boss's eye. "Deputy Director Vladimir Khachenski is here to see you, sir," she announced.

Khachenski served as Demodov's right-hand man, excelling in interrogation and physical intimidation. Khachenski harbored secrets, even from his superior. Demodov remained oblivious to Khachenski's true loyalties.

"Send him in," Demodov instructed.

Khachenski entered the room, closed the door behind him, and confidently approached Demodov's desk. His wiry physique belied his role, as he relied on henchmen for the more brutal aspects of his job. Khachenski chose not to sit in any of the office chairs, fully aware of the unspoken protocol. "We have apprehended an Englishman, Harold Harper, on espionage charges," Khachenski revealed.

"What?" Demodov exclaimed. "You've made a grave error. He's been inactive for a couple of years now."

"He was involved in a recent CIA project, and we possess substantial evidence," Khachenski replied, handing a file to the Director.

Demodov perused the file with growing disbelief and muttered, "Shept," an expression akin to "damn" or "the devil." He continued, "I considered him harmless, and look at what he's done. Is he currently in our custody?"

"Yes," Khachenski confirmed. "He's awaiting your orders."

"Begin with gentle interrogation," Demodov instructed. "I suspect he'll cooperate willingly. He strikes me as soft, unlike most British spies. If he proves resistant, resort to more forceful methods. Regardless, keep him alive until I say otherwise. I can't believe he returned to his old ways."

"As you wish, sir," Khachenski acknowledged.

After departing Demodov's office, Khachenski encountered his primary enforcer, Federov, waiting in the hallway. Khachenski pulled him aside, away from the hearing range of Demodov's administrative assistant.

"Proceed with the usual protocols," Khachenski instructed, handing the file to Federov. "Ensure he confesses to everything detailed in this dossier. First, relocate him to our clandestine facility so that only we know his whereabouts. And remember, he must remain alive, no exceptions."

Federov nodded and departed to carry out his orders.

Khachenski walked back down the hallway, passing through Demodov's reception area, where he quipped to the secretary, "Trust no man."

"Or woman, for that matter," she replied with a wry smile and a raised eyebrow.

CHAPTER 16 LANGLEY VA

In the CIA library, we spent the entire day conducting research. To maximize our efficiency, we worked individually, meticulously sifting through decades of documents, including paper records, microfilm, microfiche, and digital files gathered from thousands of agents worldwide, focusing on Bucharest. We labored tirelessly until the designated stopping time, returning to the conference room near the loading area. Despite our diligence, we still needed to compare our findings when Jerry entered.

"I've checked, and there are no ongoing efforts to track down Dascia's killer," Jerry reported.

"Did you uncover any clues about why she was killed?" I inquired.

"Not a thing," Jerry replied. "Before I share my speculations, what have you all discovered?"

"I found evidence that Dascia had collaborated with a double agent during her time in Bucharest a few years ago, and this agent mysteriously disappeared while in Moscow, just a day before Dascia was killed," Abigail disclosed. "It's likely that he's being held somewhere in or around Moscow."

"I came across an old report suggesting that when the SVR captures a spy, they typically subject them to about forty-five days of interrogation on average before executing them," Marvin added. "The report even detailed the breakdown, with roughly 14-15 days allocated for friendly questioning, followed by another 14-15 days of intense interrogation, and concluding with 14-15 days of severe torture."

"If there is a connection to Dascia's murder," I interjected, "we have approximately six weeks to locate this spy. But Dunwoody won't allow us to leave the city, let alone venture to Moscow to rescue a potentially compromised spy, without any evidence linking him to Dascia's death."

"I might have some leeway to approve a field research mission," Jerry said, a faint smirk playing on his lips as he raised his right index finger. "Our mission's sole objective would be to confirm whether such an arrest has taken place and, if so, determine the location of this spy. What's the spy's name?"

"Harold Harper," Abigail replied.

"I'm not familiar with him," Jerry admitted. "However, you must promise me that your activities will be limited strictly to information gathering through surveillance. You are to avoid any contact or engagement with Russian citizens and, certainly, do not cross paths with their intelligence services, police, or military. Act inconspicuously, like tourists or businesspeople, merely observing. Is that clear?"

"Yes," I affirmed.

"And if, by some unfortunate circumstance, any of you are captured, do not, I repeat, do not disclose your affiliation with the agency or the nature of your mission," Jerry emphasized. "You must remain silent, even if it means enduring captivity or worse. This rule is our code of honor, and if you cannot uphold this responsibility, you should reconsider your involvement."

"What will you tell Dunwoody?" I inquired.

"I'll share as little as possible, and only if he asks," Jerry explained. "I'll craft a story about taking you on a field exercise to enhance your surveillance skills. I will avoid mentioning that it's happening outside the country or related to Dascia. You'll have ten days to gather information, and then I'll pull you back."

"Will you remain here?" Jim questioned.

"Yes, it will lend credence to our cover story," Jerry confirmed. "If Dunwoody spots me around the office, he'll assume you're nearby. Remember, your primary responsibility is to inform me daily, if possible, regarding your findings and whereabouts. Jake, don't let us down."

The thought struck me—how many times had I heard that phrase before making a mistake? I quickly suppressed such thoughts; now, more than ever, I needed to demonstrate responsibility with zero room for errors.

"You were about to share your conjecture on the motive," Vincenzo reminded Jerry.

"I suspect that ex-KGB agents, who relocated to other Eastern European countries after the fall of the Iron Curtain and the end of the Cold War, are somehow involved," Jerry theorized. "I can't ascertain how Dascia became entangled with them, but her previous assignment in Bucharest might have placed her at odds with this group. We'll need to gather more information as events unfold. Understand that these agents are hazardous, and you are unprepared to confront them. If you believe you're getting within 1,000 miles of their operation, retreat immediately and inform me. By '1,000 miles,' I mean that if you venture more than 10 miles outside the center of Moscow, halt, withdraw, and contact me. Jake, I'm entrusting you to maintain control over your team and keep them out of trouble. You can book travel arrangements, and the agency will cover the expenses. Your credit cards have a $50,000 limit."

"Each?" Jenny inquired with an amused grin.

"It's for business purposes only," Abigail interjected. "No shopping sprees allowed."

"Shall we meet at our usual location tomorrow morning, then?" I suggested. "At eight AM?" Everyone nodded in agreement.

I couldn't shake the growing sense of unease. We were on the brink of a significant leap into the unknown, far from the familiar confines of our headquarters. We would be operating independently in a foreign land without understanding the motive behind Dascia's murder or how Harold Harper fit into this intricate puzzle.

CHAPTER 17 LANGLEY VA

Dunwoody stood before the desk of the CIA Director, delivering news that, while delayed, remained fresh to Rogers.

"The SVR has apprehended Harold Harper on espionage charges," Dunwoody announced.

"Is that so?" Rogers responded. "Tell me more. I thought he'd been out of the game, winding down toward retirement. Did he slip up? What potential damage could he inflict upon us? Is there any connection between him and the incident involving our trainer? Find out whatever you can about the information he might divulge. If it's possible, establish contact with him."

"He's currently in SVR custody," Dunwoody explained.

"And that's supposed to stop us?" Rogers retorted. "Think creatively."

Rogers picked up a file from his desk and added, "Also, instruct the team investigating the murder at the charity art event to explore any SVR ties related to Harper."

Dunwoody shook his head. "It's like the Cold War never really ended, isn't it?" he mused.

Rogers scoffed. "You're right."

Following his meeting with Rogers, Dunwoody proceeded to Crystal's office to check on her research progress or the lack thereof.

CHAPTER 18 WASHINGTON DC

As planned, we reconvened at our makeshift "clubhouse," our regular McDonald's meetup spot the following day. We carefully chose our roles for the upcoming trip, sticking to what we knew best. Jim Smith would assume the identity of an agriculture businessman on a quest to explore potential markets for his surplus wheat. While his family farm primarily dealt with dairy, he believed he could convincingly play the part. On the other hand, Jenny would travel as an art student, embarking on a vacation to explore Moscow's museums. Ever the computer whiz, Marvin would accompany Jenny as her tech-savvy boyfriend.

Vincenzo would slip into his preferred disguise as a Roman Catholic priest, complete with a passable knowledge of Latin, thanks to his two-year stint in a seminary. Max and I would pose as Vice Presidents of a fictitious marketing company that I'd conjured up to establish and operate U.S. franchises globally. Our focus would center on McDonald's and Burger King, as they were familiar to us, though not necessarily from a financial standpoint. We suspected that Moscow was already saturated with these franchises, which made our mission appear less enticing to any inquisitive minds and tagged us as mere newcomers.

We settled on an operational base that Abigail had uncovered during her research at Langley's library – an office supply business in Moscow conveniently operated by the CIA. This establishment, situated near the SVR headquarters, also sold art supplies, providing Jenny with a valid reason for frequenting it. The rest of us could leverage it for copying presentations or procuring supplies as needed.

In anticipation of worst-case scenarios, we prepared alternative disguises and identities to facilitate our discreet exit from the city should our cover be compromised. While I debated whether to inform Jerry of our plans, I opted to keep them classified to minimize risk. Someone within CIA headquarters had already leaked information about our training exercise to the rogue agents. Furthermore, this level of secrecy would safeguard Jerry if he weren't the leak, and we encountered difficulties. I had no intention of revealing our plans for a potential Harper rescue either.

"If we ever hope to get Harper out, we'll need a substantial amount of bribe money," I voiced my concerns. "Where do we even get that?"

Jim chimed in, "We could use our credit cards."

Ever cautious, Marvin replied, "Using our credit cards would raise red flags. They'd immediately know we've left the country."

"How much are we talking about?" Abigail inquired.

"I'd estimate around $50,000," I suggested. "What are your thoughts?"

The team exchanged shrugs and nods; no one had a better idea.

"Jerry won't ask Dunwoody for it, and I doubt Dunwoody would approve it even if he did," Marvin added.

Abigail surprised everyone with her response. "I can provide it. My trust fund deposits more money into my account monthly than I could spend in a lifetime. I lead a relatively modest day-to-day lifestyle, so that won't be a problem."

Jaws dropped, and eyes widened as her words sunk in.

"Wow!" Jenny exclaimed, capturing the sentiment of the group.

I interjected, "Once we return, assuming we're successful, you'll have to allow me to submit it as an expense to the agency."

"That's perfectly fine," Abigail agreed. "Alternatively, we could keep it as working capital."

Concerns about transporting such a substantial sum without drawing attention were raised. Vincenzo pointed out the Customs Department's requirement to report cash amounts over $10,000 when leaving or entering the country.

Marvin, shrouded in mystery, hinted at a solution. "I can handle it – getting the money out and back without detection. The fewer people who know, the better. Any inadvertent reveal at the wrong time could jeopardize our mission. Just give me the cash, and I'll return it to you within 24 hours of landing in Moscow."

Though mysterious, Marvin's proposal was met with unanimous agreement. With trust in each other being paramount, we entrusted Abigail with the task.

We dispersed, agreeing to reconvene at Langley the following morning for our last meeting with Jerry before setting off. In the meantime, we continued our efforts to perfect our disguises and strategized how to conceal them within our luggage.

CHAPTER 19 LANGLEY VA

The following day, we were gathered around the table as Jerry walked in, bearing important news.

"I've got some important news," he began. "Harper is no longer in Moscow; they've moved him to Bucharest, Romania, in case you're not up to date on your geography."

Jenny was quick to inquire, "Why the move?"

"Because Bucharest is essentially under the control of their old KGB associates. The secret police there can operate with impunity, free from the constraints of international law enforcement," Jerry explained. "They can do as they please, including torture, and no one will intervene."

I sought clarification, "So, the location has changed, but the mission remains the same, correct?"

Jerry confirmed, "That's right. I've arranged for a 'trusted friend' to provide you with unmarked transportation. This way, you won't have to go through car rental agencies, which are closely monitored. Take separate taxis from the airport to your assigned hotels. They are near each other. You can then walk from your respective hotels to the park where the car will be stashed."

Jim asked, "How will we identify your friend?"

Jerry responded, "You won't. He'll leave the car next to the park with the keys on top of the front passenger-side tire. The park is Parcul Izvor, and he'll park the car on Strada Bogdan Petriceicu Hasdeu, as close to the intersection with Strada General Ion Dragalina as possible."

I couldn't resist a quip, "Can anyone remember that?"

Jenny jumped in, reciting the details flawlessly, earning a slight double take from Jerry. Unfazed, he continued, "As a backup, you'll have it in writing."

Jerry explained, "There's a construction parking area on the west side of the intersection, across from the park. He'll attach a thin green ribbon – on the antenna if there is one, on the rear passenger door handle if not, or if neither is available, he'll roll up the right rear window with the ribbon inside to hold it in place."

Jim considered our travel arrangements, asking if we should see Cindy to make changes. However, Jerry advised against it, instructing us to make our own adjustments. He mentioned that Cindy would provide us with another set of identity papers, entry visas, and a small carry-on bag. The alternative documents would be sewn into the lining of the bags, each of them different in style to avoid drawing attention.

Jerry concluded with a stern reminder, "They're strictly a precaution. I don't expect you to need them, understand?"

We all nodded in agreement, though none genuinely believed we'd adhere to that expectation. As Jerry left the room, he popped his head back in, remarking, "I'll come to you if I sense it's time to get out," before closing the door.

I addressed the team, "I'll meet all of you at the airport tomorrow. Ensure your disguises are well-practiced and packed discreetly in your luggage. We won't put them on unless necessary."

Jenny chimed in with a surprising revelation, "In case it comes in handy, my parents were Romanian gypsies, and I grew up speaking Romanian, along with Romani dialect – we might need that."

We all regarded Jenny with a newfound appreciation for her unique background and skills. We then dispersed to collect our alternative identities and make flight reservations.

We agreed to rendezvous in two days at midnight at a peculiar bar in Bucharest known as the Crooked Cow, located in the artist colony section of the city. While we wouldn't congregate as a group, the meeting spot allowed me to confirm everyone's arrival and make any necessary adjustments to individual assignments.

Before joining the team, I decided to make a solo return trip to the research library at Langley with some personal research to conduct.

CHAPTER 20 THE VATICAN

In the heart of Rome, within the sprawling complex of the Vatican—a sovereign state in a single magnificent building—an imposing sign marked the entrance to a grand office on the second floor. It read, "Hans Cardinal Ludwig, Secretary of State." Beyond the door, a vast oval room unfolded, its perimeter adorned with a procession of desks on a rich dark-green carpet, resembling lily pads afloat on a pond. Priceless baroque paintings adorned the wall between these desks, interspersed with doorways leading to individual offices. Amidst the daily hustle and bustle, assistants diligently worked, surrounded by the typical office trappings of copiers, filing cabinets, and communication instruments.

Approximately twenty feet from the entrance, a doorway bore a shiny brass plate with the inscription, "Propagator of the Faith." This office belonged to Joseph Cardinal Mendolini, the second-largest and most magnificent within the Vatican, overshadowed only by the Secretary of State's chambers on the opposite side.

Inside, Cardinal Mendolini paced restlessly around the room, engaged in a one-sided conversation with his assistant, Archbishop Carlos Santanio, who sat nervously perched on the edge of one of the Cardinal's deep red leather office chairs. Cardinal Mendolini was a commanding figure, standing at six-foot-five, in his mid-fifties, with thinning grey hair and a robust physique that spoke of authority. Even without his scarlet robes and booming voice, he exuded an aura of dominance. In contrast, Archbishop Santanio, in his early forties, possessed a wiry frame, standing tall and lean. He could adopt a demeanor of "appropriate subservience" in the presence of the Cardinal, but beneath the facade, he was a master manipulator and strategist—a trait that Mendolini valued and utilized to his advantage.

Cardinal Mendolini had been appointed to the influential position of Propagator of the Faith two years earlier by his superior, Cardinal Ludwig, the Secretary of State, who, in turn, reported directly to Pope Ignatius II. At eighty-six years old and ailing, Cardinal Ludwig paid little attention to his subordinates, especially the ambitious Cardinal Mendolini. As a result, Mendolini operated autonomously and wielded considerable power, both within the Vatican and on a global scale.

During his two-year tenure, Cardinal Mendolini had conceived and begun executing an intricate plan to expand the influence of Christianity, particularly Catholicism, significantly. His vision for the faith matched the enormity of his ego, as he aspired to ascend to the papacy and lead the world's largest flock, regardless of the means required to achieve it. He carefully concealed his grand scheme, relying on a clandestine network of agents within and outside the Vatican to carry out his intricate plan. The Cardinal's objective was to keep his superiors oblivious to his intentions until the program was irreversibly set in motion. Once initiated, the scale of the operation would render it unstoppable, even by the Secretary of State or the current Pope.

Mendolini had discreetly recruited a substantial cohort of priests, Swiss Guard officers, and Vatican employees from within the Vatican's walls. Over time, he selected and groomed these individuals for unwavering loyalty, favoring those who displayed unwavering subservience. His inner circle was privy to specific plan details, shared on a need-to-know basis. He trusted no one beyond his closest confidants, only revealing what everyone required to fulfill their roles.

Among those aware were his assistant, Archbishop Santanio, and a select group of ex-Cold War Russian and Bulgarian spies, who had inadvertently stumbled upon fragments of Mendolini's plan while surveilling one of the Vatican's suppliers. These spies had deduced enough to jeopardize the entire endeavor if they went public, prompting Mendolini to prioritize their capture. He had dispatched agents across the globe with orders to apprehend them, dead or alive, demonstrating his willingness to flout ethical boundaries. The commandments held little sway over him.

Members of Mendolini's covert organization viewed him with a mixture of fear and admiration because he was brilliant and unhinged. Those who considered him mad learned that questioning his sanity was too perilous, given the formidable global network he had cultivated. Those who resisted his recruitment efforts vanished mysteriously. Those close to him understood that siding with the Cardinal guaranteed their survival, whereas opposing him resulted in an unquestionably terminal fate.

"The Pope appointed me Propagator of the Faith, and I interpret that as a divine directive," Mendolini declared as he continued his agitated pacing. "The Pope is infallible; his words are the voice of God. His will, as conveyed through me, is unwavering."

Archbishop Santanio voiced his reservations, "What you're about to set in motion has the potential to prematurely end the lives of millions, including many innocent people. Have you considered whether your plan meets St. Augustine's four conditions for Jus Ad Bellum, the justifications for war?"

Mendolini countered, "Certainly. Let's examine the first condition: The damage inflicted by the aggressor on the nation or community of nations must be lasting, grave, and certain. Radical Muslims have caused immense suffering, disrupted global economies, and severely restricted women's rights and freedoms. These actions undeniably meet the criteria of lasting, grave, and certain damage."

Archbishop Santanio inquired, "But have you exhausted all other means of addressing these wrongs—the second condition? And have you considered that most Muslims are not radicals?"

Mendolini argued, "How much more suffering must the faithful endure before we take decisive action to eradicate this evil? Yes, innocent lives may be lost, but my plan will ultimately eliminate this problem, with the fallen innocents becoming martyrs for the ultimate and universal expansion of Christianity."

The Archbishop cautioned, "If you are confident that your plan aligns with the mission of your office, you must then address St. Augustine's final two conditions: assuring the certainty of success and preventing the elimination of one evil from giving rise to a greater evil."

Mendolini assured, "The plan will succeed, bolstered by the latest scientific advancements. It will establish Christianity as the definitive faith across the globe. Evil shall cease to exist because Christianity will flood the world."

The Archbishop, deep in thought, said, "May God forgive us if we err."

"Amen to that," Mendolini replied confidently. "But do not fear. God is with us. Now, provide me with the latest updates on our infiltrations."

As the Archbishop exited Mendolini's office, his concerns remained unresolved, weighing heavily on his conscience.

CHAPTER 21 WASHINGTON DC

At CIA headquarters in Langley, Crystal entered Dunwoody's office, which, like her own, occupied the fifth floor in a different wing from the library where her brother was conducting research. The chances of their paths crossing were remote. Crystal avoided the loading dock area, not wanting Jake to discover her affiliation with the CIA.

Dunwoody paced behind his desk; his mind occupied with pressing matters.

"I've completed the plan for our part of the operation," Crystal said, placing a folder on his desk.

Dunwoody, looking concerned, cut straight to the point, "Who do you think killed Dascia, and why?"

Crystal responded without hesitation, "My guess would be our 'friends' at the Vatican."

Dunwoody's face lit up with agreement, "Bingo! It's a message from them. My sources indicate they collaborated with our Russian counterparts, former agents still active in Bucharest, whom Dascia had previously infiltrated and antagonized. They had a score to settle with her and seized the opportunity to send us a message simultaneously."

Curiosity piqued, Crystal inquired, "What's the message they're sending?"

Dunwoody's voice was somber as he replied, "The message is that they can reach us—me, you, and the rest of our tight-knit group in the U.S.—whenever they choose. While we're on the cusp of taking control of a significant operation, failure is not an option. If we fail, they'll eliminate us. Even if we succeed, we can never fully trust our superiors."

Dunwoody picked up Crystal's plan, outwardly disguised as a CIA operational document but far from it. "Returning to our mission," he continued, "will we have sufficient assets to ensure success with a decent margin for error?"

Crystal nodded, "Yes, and hopefully, we can keep collateral damage to a minimum."

Dunwoody's expression grew more severe than earlier, "What does that mean? We'll use any force necessary to secure control. Collateral damage is of no concern to me."

Crystal agreed, adding, "I'll transmit a coded message to Archbishop Santanio, indicating that our plan is ready."

Dunwoody acknowledged her with a curt "Okay," his mind undoubtedly occupied with the challenges ahead.

CHAPTER 22 LANGLEY VA

Upon arriving at the CIA's library, I embarked on a quest to uncover any information about my parents – a mission that extended to my sister and brother as I was also searching on their behalf. I spent many hours pursuing this elusive information until I stumbled upon a file containing their names.

With apprehension, I cautiously opened the file, finding it slim. The initial report detailed the tragic circumstances of their demise – they had been discovered lifeless in the front seat of their car, victims of gunshot wounds to the sides of their heads. Their deaths were executions.

The report said both car windows had been rolled down, implying they likely knew their assailants. There had to be at least two culprits involved because both victims appeared to have been simultaneously killed. It left me imagining a man on my father's side and a woman on my mother's, but no concrete evidence supported this theory.

Following this report, another document was marred by pages that had been torn out – a fact evident from the staples clinging to the remaining corners. However, amid the removed pages, I stumbled upon one overlooked sheet. It disclosed that the last person our parents had spoken to was an agent named Harper – the very same Harper we were soon to search for. Curiously, the document did not identify the perpetrators of our parents' execution, save for a vague "strong suspicion" that the Russians were somehow involved. There was also an enigmatic reference to "Redbird M."

Deciding to keep my discovery to myself and the knowledge of my parents' demise, I concluded that it was too premature to share such intensely personal information. I planned to delve deeper into the implications of this revelation and the mysterious developments unfolding at the Vatican.

CHAPTER 23 THE VATICAN

Archbishop Santanio, accompanied by his assistant Monsignor Pacelli, entered Cardinal Mendolini's opulent Vatican office a day later. The two ecclesiastical figures quietly stood before his desk, clutching a bundle of documents. Archbishop Santanio, though a powerful individual in his own right, invariably assumed a subservient posture in the presence of the formidable Cardinal, while Monsignor Pacelli, even more timid, appeared as meek as a mouse amidst lions. Cardinal Mendolini, confident in his near-absolute authority, second only to the Pope himself, had grand designs to expand Catholicism, believing that his divine appointment sanctioned any means necessary. However, the extent of his ambition and methods remained hidden from the Pope.

Unhurriedly, Cardinal Mendolini lifted his gaze from a book he had been perusing and inquired, punctuating his query by slamming the book onto his desk. "And what might this be?"

"Your Eminence, I have an update to report," Archbishop Santanio began, offering a report document. "In summary, the infiltration phase of your plan is nearing completion. The United States is ready, Russia is prepared, and China will be ready within a few weeks."

"Relatedly, our SVR contacts are on the brink of apprehending Harper as an extra precaution, charging him as a suspected CIA agent operating in Russia. He remains one of the few agents with the potential to lead us to Karpov's location, and we must extract this information from him."

"Additionally," the Archbishop continued, "we orchestrated the setup of a CIA agent, Gerald Wilson, as a reputed SVR spy within the United States. Subsequently, we eliminated him in a manner that has confounded the U.S. Secret Service, providing an opportunity to position one of our operatives in a critical role. Wilson's public demise occurred at a charity event in Washington, D.C."

"Is this the same Wilson who worked alongside Walenski in Panama?" Cardinal Mendolini inquired, to which Archbishop Santanio nodded in affirmation.

Cardinal Mendolini continued, "He could have potentially divulged Walenski's whereabouts. Harper remains our last hope for locating Karpov and, subsequently, Walenski. We must handle Harper with utmost care. Should he lead us to Karpov, we can extract information about Walenski's hiding place. Moreover, ascertain what Harper may know about the stolen copy of our plans."

"Of course, Your Eminence," Archbishop Santanio replied. "We are well aware of the stakes involved."

"Nothing is more crucial than locating those two traitors," the Cardinal emphasized, his eyes piercing through the room. "They possess knowledge of our plans, and should they disseminate this information to any superpower leader before our operation, our entire mission would be jeopardized."

He sternly warned, "We have discredited Karpov and Walenski, making it improbable that anyone will accept their words without the stolen copy of our top-level plans. By eliminating their contacts in France, the threat to our plans has been reduced to these two individuals and the purloined document. We must eliminate them and recover that document, or our cause could face extinction. Is that clear?"

"Yes, Your Eminence," Archbishop Santanio replied.

The Cardinal reiterated the gravity of the situation. "Harper is critical to our mission. We must find him and extract every piece of information he possesses. Remember, we cannot yet rely on the strength of our organization within the SVR to approach them directly. Handle this matter deftly."

As Santanio started to leave, Cardinal Mendolini called him back. "And send Carlotti to see me."

Upon his return, Archbishop Santanio apprised Carlotti of his mission. Carlotti was the Cardinal's most ruthless enforcer, known for his extreme cruelty. He had been recommended by prominent figures in the Sicilian and New York Mafia circles, lauded for his brutality in eliminating enemies, even torturing and killing family members in front of one another. This reputation made him a valuable asset in the Cardinal's covert operations.

"Your Eminence," Carlotti greeted the Cardinal. "What problem shall I have the pleasure of solving today?"

The Cardinal instructed him, "Locate Harper, discover his destination, and ensure we extract every piece of information he possesses regarding the whereabouts of Walenski and Karpov. We must uncover the location of his stolen copy of our plans. Do not eliminate him until we are certain that we have extracted all the information we need. Understood?"

"Of course, Your Eminence," Carlotti acknowledged. "I shall proceed immediately."

As an afterthought, Cardinal Mendolini added, "Pacelli must be held accountable for his previous blunders."

"Understood, Your Eminence," Carlotti replied with a subtle smile, anticipating the sinister tasks ahead – the disappearance of Monsignor Pacelli and a rendezvous with his Russian counterparts in the SVR, where he intended to experiment with some newly devised torturous techniques, some of which he had gleaned from encounters with Dunwoody at the CIA.

CHAPTER 24 WASHINGTON DC

At CIA headquarters in Washington, Dunwoody burst into Crystal's office, his demeanor charged with frustration and suspicion.

"I heard you were in the library," he exclaimed, his tone laced with accusation. "What were you doing there?"

Crystal hesitated briefly before responding, taken aback by the unexpected anger in his voice. Sensing distrust emanating from Dunwoody, she opted not to divulge the whole truth.

"I was researching Gerald Wilson, the spy killed at the art show," Crystal replied, carefully choosing her words. "Unfortunately, I didn't uncover any additional information."

Dunwoody regarded her with a frown, his suspicion not entirely dissipating. "I thought you might be delving into something you shouldn't be," he muttered cryptically.

Curious, Crystal inquired, "Something specific in mind?"

Dunwoody dismissed her question, his agitation gradually subsiding. "Never mind," he conceded, though not entirely convincingly.

Before he could depart, Crystal seized the opportunity. "By the way," she interjected, "what's the status of that new team Dascia was training?"

Dunwoody considered her query. "Oh, yes, the team," he replied. "Wallace has taken them out for a field exercise to hone their investigative skills."

"That's reassuring," Crystal remarked with a hint of irony. "We wouldn't want eager young agents poking around where they shouldn't."

Dunwoody nodded in agreement. "Indeed," he acknowledged before abruptly exiting her office.

Still unsettled by the unanswered questions surrounding the spy's death at the art show and Dascia's murder, Crystal couldn't shake her suspicions. She wondered if both killings were connected and the Russians were genuinely responsible, given her awareness of counterparts in the SVR. Her lingering doubts extended to Dunwoody, pondering whether he had any involvement or knowledge of the events yet remained tight-lipped. Crystal questioned whether the CIA or Dunwoody personally would take any action regarding these unsettling developments, harboring doubts that they would.

CHAPTER 25 MOSCOW

While Crystal's thoughts dwelled on the Russians, the evening sun glowed over Moscow. Khachenski had returned to the same sidewalk cafe where the SVR had apprehended Harper earlier in the day. He sat at a table, sipping coffee, accompanied by a Spanish woman. Her appearance had transformed their earlier encounter; her once-dark hair had now turned blonde. She possessed tall stature, sharp features, and a hint of an Adam's apple that betrayed her identity.

"Did he suspect anything? Did he remember a dark-haired Spanish lady setting him up?" Maria Castilla inquired.

Khachenski regarded her with a nod. "You executed it smoothly. He had no inkling of how or when the envelope appeared."

"Then, since I didn't blow my cover," she responded, "you'll be able to enlist my services again in the future, won't you?"

"When the right opportunity presents itself, certainly," Khachenski replied. "You performed admirably in Washington."

"Ah, you mean the right opportunity for this ex-Special Forces, stunning transvestite," she teased. "You should be more specific. Where did you transport the poor soul?"

"Budapest," he disclosed, concealing the actual destination, Bucharest. Trust was a scarce commodity in his line of work.

"Hungary can be quite lovely this time of year," she remarked, and they both sat in contemplative silence for a moment. He considered that Romania also had its charm.

"Well, I must attend to other matters," Khachenski stated, handing an envelope to her. Maria glanced inside, a smile forming on her lips. Any tax-free currency was a delight, but $5,000 in crisp American hundreds brought even more satisfaction. "These are genuine, right? Not from one of those German printing presses you acquired a few years ago, sold to someone, and then repossessed from the Iranians?"

"My dear," he chuckled, "whether they're real or not, if we had printed them, no one would discern the difference. Pahkah." Khachenski abruptly stood up and walked away, waving without looking back. Maria waved in return, although he had already turned his gaze elsewhere. She tucked the money into her purse and continued savoring her coffee, fully aware that Khachenski always managed to keep his hands clean, ensuring her a steady income stream.

CHAPTER 26 BUCHAREST, ROMANIA

After enduring a month of isolation in a Moscow cell with no contact from his captors, Harold Harper was finally transported to Romania under the cover of night by the same two SVR henchmen, Egor Federov and Eugeny Titov, who had initially apprehended him on Khachenski's orders. The journey took two nights, traversing back roads and including an overnight stay at an SVR "safe house."

Upon arrival, Harper was unceremoniously placed in a cold, damp cell located in the basement of an ancient building nestled in the heart of Bucharest. With its dank stone walls and floors, this subterranean cell once served as a medieval dungeon. Its sparse occupants received meager food and water rations, with infrequent visits from their captors. Harper endured this grim existence for an entire week until Carlotti, Cardinal Mendolini's chief enforcer, arrived.

Upon Carlotti's arrival, he briefed the local Romanian guards responsible for the dungeon, providing them with directives from Khachenski and some of his additional instructions. Satisfied with their commitment to maintaining security and their willingness to obey his orders, Carlotti left them to carry out their duties and departed for Rome.

Later that evening, Harper was forcibly removed from his dark, damp cell by Federov and Titov. They ushered him into a small alcove, which may have once served as a wine cellar, and seated him at a weathered wooden table set with three chairs.

"I love the smell of mold and mildew in the morning," Titov quipped.

"It's night, you fool," Federov retorted, oblivious to the reference to "Apocalypse Now."

A single candle inside an old wine bottle provided the only light source. Although the cellar had a few bare light bulbs hanging from the ceiling, Federov, with his twisted psyche, preferred the psychological contrast between the romantic ambiance of candlelight and the brutality he was about to inflict. Harper sat without handcuffs, but two well-armed guards loomed nearby.

"Why am I here?" Harper inquired.

"You know why," Federov replied. "You were conspiring to pass the design specifications of our latest fighter model, the MIG-32 Fulcrum-G, to the Americans."

"That's absurd," Harper protested. "If I were attempting such a theft, I'd pass them to MI-5, not America."

"So, you admit to trying to transmit the plans to MI-5?" Titov interjected.

"No, you idiot," Harper snapped. "I didn't say that." Titov raised his hand to strike Harper but halted when Federov signaled him to hold off.

"Fine," Federov conceded. "Give us something to charge you with, and you can start serving your sentence."

"If you think for a moment that I'd assist you in framing me, you're even more foolish than he is," Harper declared.

"We'll have little choice if you persist in being uncooperative," Federov replied, refusing to engage in further argument.

With guards flanking Harper, the two men rose and escorted him back to his cell. As the heavy door clanged shut, Federov spoke softly to the guards, ensuring Harper couldn't hear. "At three in the morning, douse him with the coldest water. We need to loosen his tongue before we proceed with the more challenging questions."

CHAPTER 27 OVER THE ATLANTIC

My team and I discreetly boarded the Moscow-bound flight, ensuring we took our seats separately throughout the plane. We had strategically chosen our locations to maintain the appearance of being unconnected. Prolonged conversations among us during the flight could inadvertently expose us to individuals with potential affiliations to the Russian government. In international espionage, many Russian diplomats who frequently shuttled between Washington and Moscow played dual roles as spies. Our predicament left us with no alternative but to treat all our fellow passengers as potential adversaries.

From my seat, I had a view of Abigail, who was positioned a few rows ahead and across the aisle. Her profile was partially visible as she conversed with a fellow traveler. I couldn't help but notice her captivating beauty and her athletic physique, a growing attraction that stirred within me. However, my unwavering commitment to ethics, instilled by my sister after she assumed responsibility for us following our parents' demise, held me back. I refused to entangle myself romantically with someone under my supervision.

My rationale extended beyond the realm of mere conflicts of interest. Entering a romantic relationship could cloud my judgment during critical moments, potentially jeopardizing our team's safety and objectives. My foremost duty as a leader was to safeguard the collective well-being of the group, and I could not afford any distractions.

The overnight flight allowed most passengers, including us, to slip into slumber as we traversed the vast expanse of the Atlantic. Over the preceding week, we meticulously adjusted our sleep schedules by waking up an hour earlier and retiring earlier each day. This gradual adaptation meant that on our departure day, we found ourselves going to bed at the unorthodox hour of 3 PM and awakening at 1 AM, perfectly synchronized with the time zone we were heading toward. Our strategy paid off as we touched down in Moscow, feeling refreshed and fully prepared for the journey ahead. The next leg of our mission would involve switching to a train, and so far, everything had gone according to plan. Yet, unbeknownst to us, challenges awaited on the horizon.

CHAPTER 28 THE VATICAN

Within the hallowed halls of the Vatican, an air of tension hung heavy as the hour approached to launch the active phase of their intricate plans. The utmost priority was safeguarding against any potential leaks in the coming months.

"Your Eminence, I've been wondering something," Archbishop Santanio broached cautiously. "What has become of Monsignor Pacelli? He has been conspicuously absent for weeks."

"He is not your concern," Cardinal Mendolini replied curtly. "Now, what is it that you want?"

"As the pieces fall into place," Santanio continued, "we find ourselves with key personnel firmly positioned within all four top security agencies. They stand ready to assume leadership positions at your command when we initiate the final stages of our plan. The time for you to give the green light on the ultimate event is drawing near."

"I've said it before," Cardinal Mendolini cautioned, "we must exercise extreme discretion within these sacred walls. Cardinal Ludwig's office is nearby, and these chambers have an eavesdropping history. If we must converse, we shall convene in the rear garden, where we can walk and speak privately. Until then, let silence be your guide within these confines."

"Of course, Your Eminence," Santanio conceded, retreating a step and offering a slight bow as he followed Mendolini down the hall towards the tranquil garden.

Once they reached the secluded garden, Santanio divulged, "Firstly, you should know we've handled the CIA training agent Harper had contacted. We believe she had insufficient time to act on the information. Furthermore, Dunwoody has assured us that the CIA team currently in training cannot launch any form of retaliation. It comprises entirely of raw recruits and poses no threat. Dunwoody also assured that no other agents would be conducting investigations."

Soon, within the confines of the garden, they would discuss the most pressing threat to their grand design. A small group of aging spies had cunningly pieced together disparate fragments of intelligence, unraveling Mendolini's intricate plans. They had even managed to secure a copy of the preliminary plans before being exposed, forcing them to flee, seeking refuge in the farthest corners of the globe. As far as Santanio and Mendolini knew, at least one of these aging spies still clung to a copy of the plans. Mendolini's operatives were currently scouring the globe, hell-bent on locating and eliminating them. For now, only Mendolini's inner circle was privy to the existence of these old spies, but that would change in due course.

CHAPTER 29 BUCHAREST, ROMANIA

In the frigid, subterranean confines of an ancient, crumbling edifice nestled deep within Bucharest, Harper found himself curled on a meager cot, his clothing clinging damply to his shuddering frame—a reminder of the nocturnal drenching he had endured. With the dawn's feeble light filtering in, a cacophony of bootsteps echoed against stone, and the grating clank of metal doors announced the arrival of his captors. Hope for sustenance and water flickered briefly before being extinguished by the sight of Titov and Federov, flanked by their unyielding sentinels. Once more, Harper was hauled to the rigid wooden chair by his unrelenting guards, bracing himself for another grueling round of questioning.

"Did you enjoy a restful slumber last night?" Federov inquired, his smile tinged with sarcasm.

"I think you're fully aware of how I slept," Harper retorted, his tone resolute.

"Perhaps you meant to say you 'slept damp'?" Titov chimed in, his laughter a solitary amusement. "Ha, ha."

"You are flagrantly violating the principles of the Geneva Convention," Harper asserted.

"Those ideals were buried in the ashes of World War II," Titov responded callously. "Only the United States and Britain ever heeded that worthless parchment."

"So, are you prepared to confess?" Federov pressed.

"Confess to what?" Harper parried.

"Confess to whatever offenses we deem appropriate," Federov replied, an air of indifference about him.

"And what might those offenses be?" Harper inquired.

"Espionage would suffice," Federov proposed.

"Espionage carries a death sentence, I believe," Harper observed.

"Yes," Titov hissed, a malevolent grin stretching across his face.

"What can you reveal about the whereabouts of your old acquaintance, Demetri Karpov?" Federov probed.

"Who?" Harper pretended ignorance.

"Don't feign ignorance," Titov snapped. "You know who Karpov is."

"Perhaps we could reduce a few years from your sentence," Federov suggested.

"A sentence for a capital offense?" Harper quipped.

"Maybe we'll commute it to life imprisonment, sparing you a few years at the end," Titov interjected.

"I have nothing to disclose," Harper maintained.

"And what about your old friend, Nikoli Walenski?" Federov continued.

"Wasn't he one of your own?" Harper deflected.

"Silence, Titov," Federov commanded. "Where is he?"

"Tell me since he's your operative," Harper countered.

"Answer my questions!" Federov snapped.

"What's in it for me?" Harper demanded.

Titov's fist clenched, halted only by Federov's restraining grip.

"How about we offer you prison time instead of a firing squad or a noose?" Federov suggested. "It would simplify matters."

"Life imprisonment in one of your notorious prisons, I assume?" Harper remarked. "I'd prefer you to end it swiftly."

"Well, we might have to account for your demise at some point," Federov explained. "Explain why you were executed without due process. We'd require a semblance of a trial or evidence of an escape attempt to avoid potential charges of crimes against humanity or other global war crimes. Moreover, someday, higher-ups in our organization might want to negotiate an exchange of informants with the CIA or MI-5, and we'd have to explain about those who disappeared while in our custody."

"Surely we can concoct a plausible explanation," Titov argued.

"If only you grasped how feeble that sounds," Harper chuckled. "Using a blatantly false confession to justify my execution? A fifth-grader could dismantle that logic."

Titov appeared irked, and Harper's subtle smile hinted at the possibility that Titov might not have advanced beyond fifth grade.

"In any case, we can detain you indefinitely," Federov declared. "Sooner or later, you'll provide us with the information we seek, or you'll languish in this cell from boredom—or pneumonia."

Federov signaled to the guards, who promptly returned Harper to his desolate cell.

"Sweet dreams," Titov jeered as they retreated, trailed by their ever-watchful sentinels.

Federov and Titov, secure in their dominion over Harper, believed that no intelligence agency of any nation would dare venture into the perilous depths where former SVR operatives thrived without the constraints of the law. Only amateurs, ignorant of the lurking perils, might dare to enter their realm, unaware of the impending danger that awaited them.

CHAPTER 30 LANGLEY VA

At Langley, Crystal grew concerned about Dunwoody's trust in her waning from his recent reticence, and her prior observations of how he distanced himself when skeptical raised red flags. She decided it was crucial to devise a strategy to rebuild his confidence in her.

Determined, she entered Dunwoody's impeccably neat and organized office and sat.

"I meant to share something with you earlier, during my research in the library regarding the Wilson assassination," she began. "I believe you'll find it quite intriguing. Unfortunately, I got sidetracked amidst our other discussions."

She handed him several loose pages she had discreetly torn out. He accepted them, arranged them, and started to read. As Crystal contemplated her plan to regain Dunwoody's trust, she had calculated that providing him with these pages posed no threat to Jake. She believed that Dunwoody wouldn't draw any connection to her past actions, especially since she had assumed her husband's last name upon marriage and had never disclosed her maiden name when joining the CIA. There was a risk that he might link the couple's surname in the reports to Jake's last name, but she was confident that his self-absorbed nature would deter him from delving too deeply into the backgrounds of those beneath his command.

"These pages allude to the termination of a double-agent couple roughly 15 years ago," she continued. "It appears they were eliminated due to concerns that they might expose the initial phases of a larger plan—the very plan that's now taking shape. It's risky to leave such potentially traceable records in our files; they should never have been included. I assume you'll ensure their proper disposal."

"Wow," Dunwoody remarked. "I'm glad you caught that. We still need to be vigilant about our plans leaking prematurely, but you did the right thing by bringing this to my attention."

Crystal watched as he finished reading and methodically fed the pages into his shredder, one by one.

"You didn't keep a copy for yourself, did you?" he inquired, his brow furrowing.

"What would I need them for?" she replied, feigning innocence. In truth, she had secured a copy discreetly.

"You're right," he acknowledged.

"It shouldn't be long before everything is set in motion," he remarked anxiously. "It's going to be the most significant event in human history. I can hardly wait."

Crystal couldn't help but consider that he might be correct if everything proceeded as planned. Neither she nor

Dunwoody had any inkling of Jake's imminent actions. Even Jerome Wallace, the trainer for Jake's team, remained oblivious to the impending developments.

CHAPTER 31 BUCHAREST, ROMANIA

We arrived in Bucharest on a cold yet sunlit late afternoon. The sky stretched clear and blue, with a scattering of white puffs. This vibrant day contrasted sharply with the city's somber Romanian architecture. Bucharest exuded an aura of danger, particularly for us. Though the Securitate had supposedly disbanded after the Cold War, the same shadowy figures persisted, operating beyond the bounds of the law.

Our strategy involved booking into separate hotels and convening every night at the Crooked Cow, locally known as "Stramba Vaca." It was an eccentric bar frequented by artists and local characters—what we'd term Bohemian in the U.S., but they were the colorful locals here in Bucharest. Most were Romanian urbanites, with a sprinkling of gypsies.

We'd chosen this bar during our research because it was supposedly run by a CIA-friendly "operative." While we couldn't entirely hide our identities from this seasoned operator, we concocted a cover story for part of our team. We were on an inconsequential training mission for International Franchising in Pittsburgh, PA. My alias would be Lincoln Thomson, the company's president.

The first evening, before my comrades arrived at the bar, I met the owner, a character known as Căpitan Bizarro—masked, caped, and flamboyantly transvestite. Despite appearances, I addressed him as a man, and he responded in kind. His English was somewhat accented and challenging to decipher.

"What shall I call you?" I asked, unsure of whether we should shake hands or hug.

"Call me Căpitan Bizarro," he replied. "And who might you be?" He extended his limp hand for a handshake, complete with purple-painted nails matching his eye shadow.

"I'm Lincoln Thomson," I replied. "President of International Franchising, based in Pittsburgh, PA."

"Okay, Mr. Thompson," he said. "But what's your real game? CIA? SVR double agent? Something else?"

"I can't say."

"No need to worry," he assured me. "No one pays much attention to me here."

I couldn't help but chuckle inwardly. Who did Căpitan Bizarro think he was fooling?

"If you must know," I said, "I've brought a couple of trainees to your historic city for their training. They're newcomers to our business, experiencing their first overseas exposure."

"And you chose Bucharest for their initiation?" he asked with a hint of amusement. "You're as daring as I am, aren't you?"

"Perhaps," I replied. "Can you point out the prison guards when they arrive? We want to assess my team's ability to gather information about their local police chief discreetly. We don't want to arouse suspicion, so a couple of us are on this task."

"Oh, really?" he said. "And why is that?"

At that moment, Jenny and Abigail entered the bar, elegantly dressed. I'd instructed them to observe the male patrons, particularly the prison guards. Căpitan Bizarro noticed the recognition in their eyes and gestured subtly toward a table where two uniformed men sat.

"You bring some attractive bait," he remarked.

I signaled to Abigail, discreetly nodding in the direction of the table.

"Their training assignment," I explained, "is to gather information about the Police Chief. We're looking for any dirt, such as payoffs or privileges, that he accepts to look the other way. If they succeed in extracting information from the guards, we might consider a more daring exercise—sneaking into the prison to photograph some documents on the Chief's desk. It's merely a test of their discretion, nothing more."

"So, you don't care if they get caught?" he asked. "They're expendable, as you Americans say?"

"Yeah," I said. "That's the idea. We'll be out of Bucharest in a week. We can't accomplish much else in such a short time."

I mainly was fabricating this story. Our actual plan was to reach the cells in the basement, and free the spy held there, intending to exit the country within three days, not seven.

Căpitan Bizarro guided me to a front table, affording me a prime view of the guards that the ladies on the stage were entertaining. As I settled in, Marvin arrived and sat at the neighboring table. He subtly patted his left pocket, indicating he had the money.

Leaning closer to ensure privacy, I asked, "How much did you manage to obtain?"

"I've got sixty grand—actually made a ten grand profit on the sale," Marvin replied.

"Sale?" I inquired. "What did you sell?"

"It was surprisingly easy," he explained. "A rare stamp concealed within the pages of the paperback book I was reading on the plane. I breezed through customs with it under my arm. I'd already found a buyer online before we left. He was eager to convert his dollars into something small, just as I wanted to do the opposite. It was a perfect trade."

We observed Jenny and Abigail in action, working to outdrink the prison guards, no small feat given their Vodka-drinking upbringing. With the aid of CIA-provided pills, they countered the effects of alcohol. One of the guards, the apparent leader, shook his keyring at Abigail, asserting his authority over the others. Before long, she held his keys and playfully teased Jenny with them. The guards, in their inebriated state, found it amusing. Jenny called for more drinks, further distracting the guards. Abigail feigned illness, covered her mouth with one hand, and dashed to the restroom. She used a small flat tin containing clay to capture impressions of each key's notches and grooves. When she returned, the guard had realized his keys were missing but, seeing them in her hand, he playfully scolded her with a wag of his finger.

With the mission accomplished, we had molds of all the keys, and no one, not even Căpitan Bizarro, was the wiser. Gradually, we all departed. The girls were able to disentangle themselves from the guards, who had succumbed to sleep aided by a couple of pills slipped into their drinks.

The following morning, our team convened at our designated meeting point on the park's east side surrounding the Parliamentary Palace. We had all arrived there by jogging or walking in from various directions, blending seamlessly with the other park-goers. To outsiders, we appeared to be nothing more than a group of joggers chatting as we stretched and warmed up. Jerry had arranged for a serviceable old limousine, which Jim had driven to the hotel and discreetly parked on the street. Abigail had successfully duplicated the keys from the molds she'd created at a local hardware store using a DIY key-cutting machine and a bit of bribery.

"Do we have confirmation that our target is in the prison?" I asked, voicing our foremost concern.

"We're quite certain," Jenny replied. "One of the guards last nights, in an attempt to impress us, mentioned they were responsible for guarding a highly important prisoner in the basement. However, he couldn't provide any further details, fearing execution."

"That will have to do," I said, sighing in relief. "Jerry told me he'll arrive tomorrow to check on our training. Our window to extract Harold Harper is tonight because Jerry would never authorize such a high-risk mission for our inexperienced team. We don't know how much time Harper has left down there. Just think about it— if one of us were trapped like that, we'd hope for a rescue, right?" Everyone nodded in agreement.

We meticulously outlined our plans for the night's operation.

At 3:00 AM, we converged on the prison from different directions. Behind the wheel of our trusty limo, Jim Smith parked as inconspicuously as possible near the guards' entrance. Despite the limo's obvious presence, he did his best not to appear out of place. Jim's appearance, that of a mid-western farm boy, didn't fit the typical image of a limo or getaway driver. He resembled the farm boys who ventured into Bucharest from the surrounding countryside in search of work during tough crop seasons, which were frequent.

When we were ready to proceed, I discreetly touched the cross hanging around my neck—a gift from Crystal carried for good luck. The darkness of the night was in our favor. Armed with Abigail's key duplicates, we quickly slipped through the guard's entrance. Jenny stayed close to me, Abigail covering our rear to secure our escape route. Max, Marvin, and Vincenzo trailed closely behind. We had to move cautiously and silently without a blueprint of the interior. Passing a corridor branching to the right, we spotted a guard dozing at his post. Soon enough, we found ourselves in a small sea of desks—the squad room, likely. No members of the squad were present.

We located an open stairwell with steps leading both up and down. The lower flight descended into what we presumed was the infamous basement. At the bottom of the stairs, a pair of thick, insulated metal doors stood, likely designed to muffle screams. Surprisingly, no guards were in sight. Descending silently, we peered through the small window in each door. Seeing no immediate threats, I began to worry that Căpitan Bizarro had betrayed us, leading us into a trap. Jenny carefully unlocked the right-hand metal door, and we cautiously pulled it open, peeking around the corner.

The primary hallway intersected right in front of our doorway, with another hallway branching to the right. I surmised that the latter corridor housed the cells. A desk was angled to give the guard a view of both hallways. Slumped behind the desk, one guard lay asleep, his head resting on crossed arms. A ring of cell keys lay atop the desk, so Jenny quietly and deftly picked them up, motioning us toward the cells.

Once again, we had to proceed with utmost stealth. Waking another prisoner and not rescuing them would lead to a cacophony that would jeopardize everyone's escape. Silently, we moved down the corridor, checking each cell for a British-looking man. No one matched the description; all the prisoners had dark hair and skin. Near the end of the corridor, we encountered a solid metal door on the right with a small window and a food slot. Dimly lit, it was difficult to discern, but we had strong reasons to believe this was Harold Harper's cell. We quietly unlocked the cell, hoping to find him asleep and not startle him. Harper was huddled in a far corner, curled up like a wounded animal. His face and hands were caked with grime and dried blood, rendering him as dark as the other inmates. He had been brutally beaten recently. The whites of his eyes shone like tiny flashlights in the darkness, radiating a fear greater than I had ever witnessed.

"Harold Harper?" I whispered. At first, Harold didn't respond, seemingly in shock.

"Yes," he eventually replied weakly.

"We've come to get you out of here," I assured him.

Harold seemed incapable of making the journey to the limo, let alone the long trip home. He didn't react to the instructions I provided. Max and Marvin helped him to his feet, his legs resembling rubber, requiring our constant support. We retraced our steps back through the metal doors, arriving at the top of the stairs without being detected. Just as we were about to exit the squad room, we heard footsteps descending from above.

I quickly decided to hide or dash through the squad room to the opposite corridor. I chose the latter. With my pistol drawn, I followed the others in case we needed it. I hadn't expected to see who was descending the stairs. To my surprise, Căpitan Bizarro stood surrounded by a dozen heavily armed policemen and an officer. My heart pounded as I strained to hear their Romanian conversation, hoping Jenny was picking up on their dialogue. With little time to spare, Jenny and I swiftly turned and hastened down the hallway, slipping through the guard's door held ajar by Abigail before gently closing it.

Stepping out into the cool night air was invigorating. We piled into the limo, with Jim at the wheel, and carefully laid Harold on the floor. I sat beside him, offering some comfort.

"It seems Căpitan Bizarro betrayed us," Jenny said, sharing the unfortunate truth. "They were waiting for us, but apparently on the top floor, not in the basement."

"He's become a liability to the organization," Abigail remarked.

"I'll report what transpired to Jerry," I said, "and let him decide how to handle Căpitan Bizarro."

My ruse involving the police chief's desk had bought us the crucial time we needed. It wouldn't be long before they discovered the missing spy, prompting an immediate manhunt. I shined a flashlight on Harold's face, revealing the extent of his injuries. He appeared so battered and fragile that I couldn't help but worry about whether he would survive. I turned the light away from his eyes, allowing him some respite.

"We're friends," I told him gently. "Can you share anything about why they imprisoned you?"

In slow, labored words, Harper managed to convey his urgent message, his voice weak with the gravity of the situation. "I don't have much time... I must trust you are Americans, loyal to your country. Listen carefully. There's a global conspiracy aiming to control the world. It's urgent that you stop it. Intelligence agencies are compromised. A new extranational organization is taking over. Two old spies know more. One is Nikolai Walenski. He's hiding somewhere up the Amazon near Tabatinga. The other is Demetri Karpov. You'll find him in Akutan, a small village in the Aleutian Islands. Please don't give away their locations, or they're dead. They are the last two who can lead you to the plans describing the conspiracy, and, hopefully, those plans will reveal those behind them."

"What is the conspiracy?" I asked, eager for more information. But Harper's strength waned, and he collapsed.

"Shoot me in the head now..." he whispered with his last breath and then passed away. The opportunity to inquire about my parents had slipped through my fingers.

A profound sadness washed over me as I checked for any lingering pulse, but there was none. "Did you get those names, Jenny?" I asked.

"Yes, Nikolai Walenski, Tabatinga, Amazon, Demetri Karpov, Akutan in the Aleutians," she affirmed.

"What should we do with his body?" Abigail inquired.

"First, I'm going to follow his last request and shoot him in the head," I replied. "I'll leave the gun in his hand to make it look like a suicide."

"Why?" Abigail questioned.

"He believes it will mislead those who find his body and buy us some additional time," I explained.

"You should wait until we're on a less populated street," Abigail suggested. "Turn here, Jim."

Once Jim veered onto a deserted street, I retrieved my firearm and complied with Harper's final wish. It wasn't a task I relished, but it was a sound strategy. As the team's leader, I couldn't burden one of the others with such a grim responsibility.

"Everyone, it's nearly dawn," I said. "We'll abandon the limo and set it ablaze. Fire won't erase all traces of his body, but it will delay identification. Jim, drop us off near our respective hotels. Vincenzo, accompany Jim. Discard the car close to your accommodations and ignite it. Then, and this applies to all of us, make your way to your hotels swiftly, and once inside, promptly check out. Notify the front desk that you must retrieve something from your rooms one last time. While there, transition into your disguises and take all your previous clothing with you. Exit via a side entrance, find a trash can or dumpster at least two blocks away, and dispose of your old attire."

"Where should we reconvene?" Marvin inquired.

"We'll rendezvous at Casa Capsa—a coffee house on Victory Avenue," I answered. "It's one of the oldest restaurants in Bucharest. We'll have breakfast there and wait for Jerry. I'll arrange a message to reach him with our meeting location."

"Are you planning to brief him on our activities?" Max questioned.

"That's a decision I'll need to weigh carefully," I responded. "When Jerry arrives, follow my lead, and remember to maintain your cover with your disguises."

After being dropped off individually, Jim and Vincenzo drove away in the limo. I wasn't entirely confident about their methods for ditching the vehicle and setting it on fire, but trust is the foundation of teamwork. You assign a task and have faith in your team members to carry it out.

We had all gathered in the cafe the following day before Jerry's arrival. He had landed on an early flight and was ready for breakfast. Once we had seated ourselves and placed our orders, Jerry remarked on our subdued demeanor.

"Cats got your tongues?" Jerry quipped, revealing his age.

"Just the early hour," Marvin replied, attempting to deflect attention.

Then, Jenny was drawn to a small television behind the counter. Intrigued, I turned to look as well. "What are they saying?" I inquired.

"It appears there was a major fire at a gas station, and a limo was present at the pumps when the fire erupted," Jenny relayed.

I exchanged glances with Jim and Vincenzo, who seemed a bit sheepish. They had determined that merely igniting the limo's upholstery wouldn't suffice, leading to the unintended torching of an entire gas station. While I mentally applauded their thoroughness, Jerry interjected.

"I received word from one of our sources that the captured spy, Harper, went missing last night," Jerry informed us. "Is there anything you might know about that?"

"Our understanding is that he passed away recently," I replied.

"And how are you so certain of that?" Jerry inquired.

"We spent part of the evening at Căpitan Bizarro's establishment, which, by the way, is operated by a double agent working for the other side," I revealed.

"We had always suspected as much," Jerry acknowledged. "What else did you discover?"

"What can you tell us about Nikolai Walenski and Demetri Karpov?" I questioned.

"Stay far away from anything related to them," Jerry cautioned. "Multiple contracts are out on both, placed by the SVR and us."

"Why?" I probed.

"They share a connection of some sort—counterspies, it's believed," Jerry disclosed. "I'm not privy to the details, but I know that powerful individuals want them eliminated for some reason."

"We heard they might possess critical information regarding global security," I said.

"What kind of information?" Jerry inquired.

"That's the quandary—we don't have the specifics," I admitted. "We plan to split the team to follow leads, locate these individuals, and extract more information."

"How did you come across this information?" Jerry pressed.

"A dying man confided in us," I explained.

"And you believe it to be true because, of course, a dying person never lies," Abigail added with a touch of irony.

Jerry gave both of us a skeptical look. "So, are you suggesting we vacate this second-tier locale and seek safer surroundings?" he queried.

"That seems to be the prudent course of action," I affirmed.

"I'll be returning to Langley," Jerry declared. "Keep me fully informed—absolutely everything this time. I believe this untamed bunch no longer requires further training. However, exercise extreme caution, for I won't be able to come looking for you. And, just so you're aware, information regarding the assassination of your previous trainer, Dascia, seems to indicate the involvement of a mysterious independent organization. None of the known security agencies appear to know about it."

We hastily finished our breakfast, settled the bill, and went to the airport in separate taxis.

CHAPTER 32 OVER THE ATLANTIC

Seated in the comfort of business class on a United Airlines 747 en route to New York, Abigail and I huddled to discuss our freshly formulated plan. We discreetly shed our disguises at the airport and expertly repacked our luggage before checking in. Marvin had divided the funds, so we carried $9,999 - a dollar under the mandatory reporting threshold for traveling into or out of the United States.

Our plan laid out the subsequent stages of our mission. Half of our team would journey to the Amazon to contact Walenski, while the other half would go to the Aleutian Islands for a rendezvous with Karpov. We would tread cautiously, not revealing our true purpose, and employ the requisite evasive tactics to ensure that we weren't being trailed. Upon landing in Washington, D.C., we would be expected to proceed to our respective residences, but we had no intention of doing so. We'd spend the night at an airport hotel to disrupt any predictable patterns before catching our next flights. Our utmost priority was safeguarding the safety of these two men, as the world's two largest spy networks were hunting them. We had no intention of capturing or harming these spies; our mission was to unearth the nature of the conspiracy that had driven them into hiding, a conspiracy for which two lives had already been forfeited. Marvin had identified a small two-star hotel in Paris as our rendezvous point, chosen for its proximity to Moscow and Bucharest, which we anticipated would be crucial in our next steps.

Abigail and I conversed in hushed tones as we mapped out our strategy. "Harold made it clear that we're facing an imminent threat," I began. "I've decided to split the team - to reach both destinations simultaneously and save time. It also gives us a backup plan in case one half encounters difficulties."

"I agree," Abigail concurred. "Who do you want me to take?"

"You'll lead Max and Vincenzo, and I'll take Marvin, Jenny, and Jim," I replied. "This way, we each have a blend of strength and intelligence, in addition to our skills, of course."

"Are we departing directly from JFK once we land?" she inquired.

"Yes, but only after a night at the Holiday Inn near the airport to book flights and catch up on some much-needed sleep," I explained. "You don't have any pressing commitments elsewhere, do you?"

"No," she replied. "Do you find it unusual that none of the team are married or have significant others? Did you select the team with that in mind?"

"Not intentionally," I said. "I think the CIA tends to attract individuals who are unattached."

"Sort of like the French Foreign Legion?" she mused.

"Perhaps," I admitted. "And maybe, once this is all over, you and I can find some time to get to know each other better."

"Are you hitting on me on a delayed schedule?" she teased, flashing a smile. "You're a bit peculiar."

Her remark had me smiling as well. "On a more serious note," I continued, "what do you think we're getting ourselves into by pursuing these spies?"

"If an independent group indeed killed Dascia," she pondered, "then we're faced with questions such as: How extensive is this organization? Who is pulling the strings, what are their objectives, and what are they planning? We must glean answers to these questions from these spies."

Unbeknownst to us, Moscow was alarmed over our audacious actions as we sped toward America.

CHAPTER 33 MOSCOW

In Moscow, Khachenski sat before SVR Director Leonid Demidov's imposing desk, a bold move that few dared to make.

"Why would they shoot Harper in the head after going to all the trouble to free him?" Demidov inquired, his stern gaze fixed on Khachenski.

"It's rather peculiar that they waited until they had him in the limo," Khachenski mused. "Perhaps they lacked a silencer and didn't want to reveal their presence at the police station."

"And you claim to have been on the third floor while they were in the basement, correct?" Demidov probed.

"We received information that they intended to ransack the chief's records on the third floor," Khachenski responded.

"Where did you obtain this information?" Demidov pressed.

"Captain Bizarro informed us that he had overheard their plans," Khachenski replied.

"Perhaps they manipulated him, leading him to believe that was their objective," Demidov speculated. "Or maybe he was complicit in their scheme."

"Either way, his usefulness is now in question," Khachenski admitted.

"Well, it still doesn't explain why they eliminated Harper after freeing him," Demidov remarked.

"That may remain a mystery," Khachenski conceded. "We will continue our investigation. Is there anything else?"

Demidov dismissed him with a dismissive wave of his hand. Khachenski promptly rose and exited the office.

Returning to his office, Egor Federov, his trusted right-hand man, joined him.

"Egor, they killed Harold Harper after breaking him out of his cell," Khachenski revealed. "And I believe I know the reason."

"Why?" Federov inquired.

"They released him to extract certain information," Khachenski explained.

"Information about what?" Federov probed.

"Our plans," Khachenski said cryptically.

"The Vatican's plans, you mean?" Federov whispered cautiously.

"Lower your voice, you fool," Khachenski hissed. "Yes, that's what I mean."

"What did Harper know?" Federov asked.

"I'm uncertain, but wasn't he acquainted with Nikolai Walenski?" Khachenski inquired. "The American spy who infiltrated our ranks for over a year before we apprehended him?"

"The same U.S. spy we've been pursuing for twelve months?" Federov clarified.

"Exactly," Khachenski affirmed. "Walenski poses the gravest threat to our plans, along with Dmitri Karpov. Should either of them manage to establish contact with high-ranking officials in any government, many of us will face execution, including you and me. Now, assemble your team and track down Walenski and our missing spy, Dmitri Karpov. They may be working together, or at the very least, they possess information about each other's whereabouts. They held each other in high regard despite being on opposing sides. Go, handle this discreetly! And don't eliminate one of them until you've extracted the other's location."

"Yes, sir," Federov acknowledged before departing the office, his mind filled with questions about the enigmatic killers of Harper and their mysterious agenda.

CHAPTER 34 WASHINGTON DC

Upon landing, retrieving our luggage, and clearing customs, we headed straight to the Holiday Inn in dire need of rest. Returning to our regular lives immediately was out of the question for three compelling reasons. Firstly, we had reason to believe that individuals from Bucharest might be in pursuit of us. Secondly, the task of booking our flights lay ahead. And lastly, there was pressing work that demanded our attention.

Before boarding our flight the following morning, I dialed Jerome's number.

"They nearly got me during my return to the States," he disclosed urgently. "This call must be brief, so pay close attention. Utilize only public phones. Place trust solely in your team. Cease communication with this office until either you or I unravel this mystery. Keep us posted whenever possible using encrypted messages. The threat emanates from within our organization. Exercise extreme caution. I'll be out of touch for a while."

The line abruptly went silent, and I could only hope it was because Jerome had hung up. He had always been a stalwart ally, but his voice sounded unwell. Jerome was one of those rare mavericks who could navigate the flexible channels within an otherwise rigid and conventional establishment. We found ourselves with no one left to trust, and our list of adversaries remained uncertain. We were confident that some individuals in Moscow were displeased with our actions, but the extent of our unknown enemies remained a daunting enigma.

We departed for Manaus via Miami while Abigail and her team embarked on their journey to Alaska.

CHAPTER 35 WEST ALEUTIANS, ALASKA

Abigail, accompanied by her small team of Max Johnson and Vincenzo Bianchi, reached Anchorage after a lengthy journey spanning half the globe. Upon arrival, they promptly secured a flight to Unalaska, an Aleutian island approximately 800 miles west of Anchorage. To minimize the chances of being tracked, they intentionally booked the second available flight after touching down.

Their next leg of the journey brought them to Unalaska after a three-hour flight in a Saab 340 turboprop. Once they arrived, they took a brief taxi ride to Dutch Harbor, a quaint seaport town, where they intended to arrange for a seaplane to transport them to Akutan. However, to their disappointment, they were turned away due to adverse weather conditions. While the weather seemed manageable to them, they respected the stories they had heard about the unpredictable nature of Bering Sea weather. The seaplane base agent suggested an alternative – the Lady Di fishing vessel. Abigail interpreted this recommendation as indicating that the expected weather problem was related to low-lying cloud cover rather than severe storms.

Reluctantly, they approached the Lady Di, an aging and dilapidated fishing vessel. After gaining permission to come aboard, they were escorted to the ship's captain, a rugged-looking Russian named Sergei Popov, who agreed to transport them to Akutan. The ship's captain possessed a dense beard that matched the hair on his arms and chest, giving him an imposing appearance. While the 20-minute flight to Akutan would have been routine in a Grumman G21 Goose seaplane, they now faced a three to four-hour journey on this less-than-reliable vessel.

The Lady Di, measuring 160 feet in length and 50 feet in width, with a shallow draft of twelve feet, left Abigail with concerns about its seaworthiness for the turbulent Bering Strait. She recognized that their safety would hinge more on the captain's experience than the ship's condition. Abigail attempted to engage the captain in a conversation about Akutan, but he displayed little interest in communicating beyond inquiring why they were headed there. She fabricated a story, telling him they were government fisheries inspectors. Curiously, the captain did not request to see identification to support her claim, leading her to believe that it didn't particularly matter to him. However, he offered a few cabins for their use if needed during the trip, an offer Abigail declined, anticipating that the journey would be completed within four hours.

The outbound trip proved to be rocky but not excessively turbulent. Contrary to what Abigail was told by the seaplane operator, the skies soon cleared, raising her suspicions. During the voyage, one of the crewmen informed Abigail that Trident Fisheries was the sole active business in Akutan. It was one of the largest seafood processors, dealing with crab, cod, and pollock and converting them into various frozen fish products. Most of the town's residents worked at the factory seasonally, with only a few staying year-round.

Upon their arrival, the shoreline was bustling with hardworking men, their lives colored by the dark and ominous atmosphere of the sea and sky surrounding them. Abigail, possibly the only woman on the island, felt a sense of unease but took comfort in the presence of Max and Vincenzo. They had agreed with the ship's captain to spend four hours in Akutan before their return trip to Unalaska, underlining the captain's insistence on a tight schedule and advance payment.

To disembark, the captain arranged for a small boat to transport them ashore. As they approached the dock, two sailors produced pistols from beneath their shirts, instructing them to leave their weapons behind due to a local policy prohibiting firearms. Abigail suspected otherwise but decided against confrontation. Max and Vincenzo reluctantly surrendered their pistols, with a request for their return in the same condition they were given.

Stepping onto the dock, they knew they couldn't directly inquire about Demetri Karpov since he was hiding and using an alias. They proceeded up a muddy road, the only street in the small village. The village stretched around the base of a rounded, bald lava mound, rising over 1,000 feet from the sea. The habitable area was limited, while the island spanned approximately 14 square miles. The village comprised around 30 residences, while the fishery operation was across the harbor on the western shore. Despite being a Sunday, the fishery was closed, due to the absence of fishing ships for unloading and processing.

Curious locals emerged from their homes as they walked along the street or peeked out to observe the newcomers. Abigail and her team scanned the faces, hoping to spot any distinctive signs that would lead them to the old spy. Some men openly carried holstered pistols, contradicting the alleged local policy. Abigail and her team felt like goldfish in a small bowl, surrounded by curious cats.

During their initial pass, they failed to identify anyone who stood out. Abigail methodically began eliminating houses where no one had come out to observe them. On their return pass, Vincenzo halted Abigail and gestured toward a young woman discreetly watching them from a partially opened door. Abigail realized she wasn't the only woman on the island. She and Vincenzo stopped while Max, initially oblivious, continued on and then had to jog back to rejoin the other two. The young woman closed the door almost entirely but continued to peer out. Abigail moved closer, allowing her to speak in hushed tones.

"Do you know a man named Demetri?" Abigail inquired. The woman scrutinized her for a prolonged moment, her single visible eye observing Abigail through the narrow gap between the door and the frame.

"Who are you?" she eventually asked.

"We're friends," Abigail replied. "My name is Abigail."

"What do you want?" the woman queried.

"We need to ask him a question of great importance," Abigail explained.

"What question?" the woman pressed.

"I'm afraid it's something only he can answer," Abigail conceded. The woman continued to study them before slightly widening the door, tilting her head to indicate a house diagonally across the street. Abigail expressed her gratitude.

Abigail, Max, and Vincenzo crossed the street, approaching the house shrouded in secrecy. All the windows were concealed behind blinds, and no signs of life existed. Abigail knocked on the door and waited but received no response. She knocked once more, but the silence persisted.

"I know you're in there," she asserted. "We need to talk urgently."

A soft "Go away" emanated from the inside.

"Please," Abigail implored. "Harper sent us. It's crucial."

After a prolonged silence, shuffling sounds emerged from within, and the door latch clicked, though the door remained shut. Abigail cautiously pushed it open, with Max and Vincenzo following closely. The room was dimly lit, revealing only one discernible object in the ample space – the gleam of a metallic replica of the Eiffel Tower.

"Whoa," Abigail exclaimed. "We've come unarmed."

"You were armed," he retorted. "What do you want?"

Abigail noticed a telescope by the window and detected an Eastern European accent with a hint of Italian lilt in his voice.

"We were sent to you by Harold Harper," she said, emphasizing his last dying words.

"And you've also brought death upon me," he sighed. "They'll know you came here."

"Who will?" she inquired.

"You're ignorant of everything, yet you've exposed me," he stated. With a resigned tone, he continued, "But it was only a matter of time. Besides, you lack the resources as a group. You're like helpless infants, Babes in the Woods ill-prepared for the task ahead. I'm wasting my remaining breath on you."

"Who, what, and when are we talking about?" Abigail pressed.

"It will get you killed too," he warned.

"We'll take that chance," Vincenzo interjected.

"The little man talks brave," he remarked. "I wish I'd live long enough to see him eat those words."

As their eyes adjusted to the dim light, Abigail discerned that the object in his hand wasn't a gun but a metallic replica of the Eiffel Tower. A framed print of the Mona Lisa hung on the wall, suggesting a special connection to Paris.

The elderly spy sat with his hands folded in his lap, initially conveying anger but revealing resignation and sadness. Abigail began to suspect they had made a mistake by approaching him openly.

"What do we need to know?" she asked.

"I'll tell you, though it probably won't do you any good," he replied. "Find the priest Rodolphe in Paris and look for a message on his body. But beware; the forces you're up against are beyond your imagination, greater than the world has ever seen. You're entirely outmatched. Good luck. If you make it that far, finding the message will lead you deep into their lair. Trust no one, especially anyone in the intelligence community – they've been infiltrated, possibly at the highest levels."

"What kind of message?" Max inquired.

"We have no more time," Demetri said. "Leave now while you can."

Abigail wanted additional information, but his clenched jaw indicated he wouldn't divulge further details. The three departed and heard a muffled gunshot as they walked away. Vincenzo and Max turned to look back, but Abigail continued walking. Afterward, they hurried to catch up with her, sneaking another glance over their shoulders.

"Did you expect that?" Vincenzo asked.

"He knew it was inevitable," she responded. "And he realized we had exposed him, leaving him with no escape from this remote corner of the earth. He was at the end of his rope."

Abigail felt anger over their mission's unintended consequences, resulting in the old spy's demise – someone who merely sought to spend his remaining years in peace. She also resented their lack of control over their current predicament, relying on someone she couldn't trust to ensure their safety. Her apprehensions were well-founded, and she was frustrated with herself for falling for the false assurances of the seaplane service operator.

Upon returning to the captain's ship, they found the sailors standing in the boat, looking up the street, having heard the muffled gunshot. When Abigail requested their firearms, the sailors merely shrugged and gestured toward the ship.

As they resumed their voyage, Abigail and her team discussed their limited findings from the journey and their concerns about the escalating fatalities surrounding them. They eagerly anticipated their return to the rendezvous point.

The weather remained overcast, with rough waters and no land in sight. They had been sailing for more than five hours now, whereas their initial journey to Akutan, against the current, had taken less than four hours.

"It's midnight," Abigail remarked.

She needed to learn the captain's destination. She hoped to disembark from the ship before reaching wherever he intended.

"Let's retreat to the cabins they assigned us and rendezvous on the stern deck in an hour. That should reduce any suspicion. Then we'll attempt to commandeer one of their lifeboats."

At 1 AM, the trio reconvened on the aft deck, free from crew interference. Silently, they began releasing one of the lifeboats. Vincenza spotted something in the distance.

"Look, a light," he pointed. "We can aim for that. The sea is getting choppier."

Undetected, they launched the boat and rowed feverishly, taking turns to sustain their relentless pace.

As they approached the distant light, they realized it wasn't on an island but a smaller fishing vessel. Abigail called out, "Ahoy, who's aboard?"

A greasy head emerged from a hatch. "What the…?" the ship's captain and sole crew member muttered.

"May we come aboard?" Abigail asked.

"Who are you? Where did you come from? Are you from that trawler that just passed?" the captain inquired.

They swiftly climbed aboard.

"I'm Abigail, and these are Max and Vincenzo. Yes, we had to leave that ship; we didn't feel safe," Abigail explained.

"I'm Jackson," the captain replied. "I can understand that. There are unsavory characters in these waters."

Abigail noticed the grease on Jackson's hands, asking, "Is your boat operational?"

"It should be once I reinstall the carburetor."

"Hey, is it just me, or is that trawler heading back this way?" Max pointed out.

"Can we extinguish that light until you fix the boat?" Abigail inquired.

"Only if I can make the repair blind, which I don't recommend," Jackson replied, shielding the light with a bucket.

"If you get it running, can you outrun that ship?" Vincenzo asked, pointing.

Jackson descended into the engine compartment. Moments later, he shouted, "This rig will outpace anything around once I get her running."

They watched as the trawler altered its course, heading directly toward them. Tension mounted as it approached.

"Are you nearly finished?" Vincenzo inquired.

"Another three or four minutes should do it," Jackson hollered from below.

"That's cutting it close," Max observed.

Finally, Jackson emerged from the engine compartment and hurried to the wheelhouse, repeatedly cranking the engine as the trawler drew nearer. The engine roared to life, and their boat shot away like a rocket, veering in the opposite direction to the trawler's path. They passed the ship a few hundred yards to starboard. Although they noticed gunfire flashes, they remained unconcerned, as the shots were off target.

They sailed for four hours until they spotted Unalaska on the horizon at dawn. Grateful for Jackson's help, they rewarded him generously for his gallant service. Afterward, they rushed to the airport, eager to leave town before the trawler's potential return or any radio messages from its captain's contacts. They spared no expense to expedite their departure, anxious to reunite with the other half of their team and share their findings. Neither group had information about the Vatican's current situation.

CHAPTER 36 THE VATICAN

Cardinal Mendolini sat alone on an ornate lawn bench at the heart of a Vatican garden, savoring the serenity. Archbishop Santanio appeared, leading a delegation of men, each representing one of the three superpowers essential to the Cardinal's covert, global organization—an integral part of his ambitious agenda.

Behind each man followed a seminarian, bearing a lawn chair for their respective leaders. The chairs were arranged in a graceful arc, all facing Mendolini. Those who took their seats included Archbishop Santanio, Darien Dunwoody, Vladimir Khachenski, and the newest addition, Jinn Quang, the second in command of the MSS intelligence agency—China's counterpart to Khachenski and Dunwoody. Dunwoody held sway over the U.S., the U.K., and Europe, while Khachenski exerted his influence over Russia and Eastern Europe.

Mendolini had orchestrated the ascension of these organizational leaders, positioning them as seconds in command, primed to assume control of their respective intelligence agencies upon the "unexpected sudden death" of their agency heads—events that would unfold at Mendolini's bidding. This clandestine network granted him control over the intelligence apparatuses of major world powers, enabling him to manipulate their governments according to his meticulously devised schemes. Soon, he would have enough dominion to wield the world's major governments like marionettes.

As the seminarians disappeared, Mendolini began to speak. "You are pivotal to the success of our plan, and it has come to my attention that you are losing control in your areas of responsibility," he stated.

"For instance, Mr. Khachenski, can you explain how an inexperienced CIA team infiltrated your operation in Bucharest and extracted your captive, Harper—a source of critical information we required?"

"He died soon after," Khachenski responded.

"You conveniently omit that it was staged to appear as if he took his own life," Mendolini retorted. "Our concern is what Harper managed to divulge to the group of supposedly inexperienced recruits who liberated him and their subsequent actions. What do they intend to do with the intelligence they acquired?"

"We will regain control shortly," Khachenski assured.

"Mr. Quang," Mendolini continued, "Welcome to our fold. I hope you will learn from recent mishaps and avoid repeating them. Your directive is to subtly nudge your military into reallocating resources toward your western borders."

"As for you, Dunwoody, your task was to locate Walenski and Karpov. What transpired?" Mendolini queried. "Your rogue team interrogated Harper without your knowledge, likely uncovering the whereabouts of Walenski and Karpov. Moreover, they either killed Harper or abetted his suicide, erasing our best opportunity to extract valuable information."

"We will retrieve them shortly," Dunwoody replied. "Once they're in our custody, we'll extract everything they know about Karpov and Walenski. We'll squeeze every last detail from them."

Mendolini smiled, questioning, "Do you already know your team's whereabouts?"

"Not yet, but we've deployed all available resources to locate them," Dunwoody said.

"Does that sound like control to you?" Mendolini inquired sternly. "The time to deliver is now. We launch in less than 90 days, and you must regain firm control of your organization. Prepare to guide your governments according to our plans—no more errors. Is that clear? Return to your organizations and prepare for the imminent launch. You'll receive the signal in six to eight weeks."

With that, Cardinal Mendolini rose, the others followed suit in deference, and he departed into the garden, leaving Dunwoody apprehensive. He wasn't in control, and if his superior, Rogers, caught wind of the situation,

Dunwoody's fate was sealed figuratively and literally. The entire operation teetered on the brink of collapse.

CHAPTER 37 LANGLEY, VA

A week later, Randall Rogers, the esteemed Director of the CIA, sat resolutely behind his imposing desk. Dunwoody, his trusted confidant, occupied the chair before him.

"You're suggesting that the new team, originally dispatched for training in D.C., may have been involved in springing Harper and, even more astonishingly, in his demise?" Rogers inquired, his brows furrowing. "That defies all reason."

"Regrettably, I hold Wallace accountable for this," Dunwoody asserted. "I'm constrained to await his recovery."

"Yes," the Director acknowledged. "I've been informed of his unfortunate assault at the airport parking lot upon his return from Bucharest. Have you determined the assailant?"

"Not yet" Dunwoody replied. "We've established that an assailant attacked him from the backseat of his vehicle and, providentially, fled before completing the act. Wallace drove himself to a nearby gas station and called for assistance."

"I've deployed continuous security personnel outside his hospital room," Rogers disclosed. "For now, he's shielded from the consequences I would have imposed for permitting that team to exit the country and execute such a perilous, unauthorized operation. It was unauthorized, was it not?"

Dunwoody couldn't help but feel dismayed by the news of Wallace's protection.

"Indeed," Dunwoody confirmed.

"They were not even aware of Harper's identity, and he's British, for heaven's sake," Rogers remarked. "So, why would they risk liberating Harper and subsequently eliminate him?"

"I cannot fathom it," Dunwoody admitted. "I am in the process of summoning the team to unravel this mystery."

"Have they not returned yet?" Rogers inquired. "Where are they?"

"Well, we're uncertain," Dunwoody admitted. "They disembarked at JFK but may have caught another flight under different aliases. And, before you inquire, we cannot trace their whereabouts or activities at this juncture. It appears that the files containing their alternate identities have been misplaced."

"Locate them expeditiously and apprise me upon success. Bring them back posthaste!" Rogers commanded with a sweeping gesture.

Dunwoody returned to his office, where Al Kowalski, his devoted aide, awaited.

"Your operative committed a grievous blunder with Wallace," Dunwoody chided. "A mere knife attack? An incomplete mission? Truly? Let us hope Wallace did not catch sight of your operative's face."

Kowalski hung his head in embarrassment.

"Have you located Rhodes and his team yet?" Dunwoody demanded.

"Not as yet, but we are diligently pursuing leads," Kowalski assured.

"That is not satisfactory," Dunwoody retorted. "Ramp up your efforts and find them immediately."

"What is the significance of their capture?" Kowalski inquired.

"They possess knowledge," Dunwoody disclosed. "I suspect they gleaned vital information from Harper regarding the whereabouts of Walenski, Karpov, or both. While you search for Rhodes, watch for those two individuals perched atop our clandestine most-wanted list."

"One final question: do we conclude the Wallace matter?" Kowalski queried.

"No," Dunwoody replied firmly. "He is presently under strict surveillance and not going anywhere. I intend to exact our retribution in our fashion. When you locate Rhodes and his team, make them vanish discreetly, but only after extracting every morsel of information they possess."

"Understood," Kowalski acknowledged before hurrying out of the office.

Fortunately for Jake and Abigail, neither Dunwoody nor Kowalski knew Jake and his compatriots' whereabouts.

CHAPTER 38 THE AMAZON RIVER, MANAUS, BRAZIL

While Abigail, Max, Vincenzo, and I traversed the vast expanse of the Aleutian Islands, Jim, Jenny, Marvin, and I embarked on a quest to navigate the enigmatic Amazon River. Our journey led us to Manaus, where we landed after a connecting flight from Miami that lasted five hours. Upon arrival, we transported our luggage to a local bank, modest in size yet equipped with substantial safe deposit boxes. Here, we securely stowed our belongings in multiple containers and prepaid the rent for an entire year. Fortunately, one of the bank's employees was proficient in English, facilitating our transaction. Additionally, we entrusted about half of our financial resources to their care.

Subsequently, we ventured to a quaint marina alongside the river in search of vessels willing to transport passengers upstream. Regrettably, the only option exceeding a modest outboard boat was a timeworn wooden craft, undoubtedly in its fiftieth year. It bore an uncanny resemblance to the vessel immortalized in Humphrey Bogart's cinematic classic, "The African Queen." A seasoned mariner lounging beneath the boat's shaded canopy caught my attention as I approached.

As I soon discovered, this individual held the position of captain, sporting a prodigious, grizzled beard that could have rivaled Ernest Hemingway's. Despite his apparent non-native origin, his impeccable command of

Portuguese became evident as I overheard his directives to a crew member. His body bore the marks of ancient tattoos, remnants from his earlier military service. Although I scrutinized them for English text, they contained only intricate designs. The boat mirrored its captain's weathered appearance, its surface marred by the ravages of time, featuring corroded steam engines, fittings, and anchors, testimony to the unforgiving Amazonian climate. If it were mine, I mused, I would lavish it with fresh paint and lacquer to extend its precarious existence.

The sole deckhand we encountered seemed to be a youthful, wiry figure, his complexion dark as a prune, brimming with nervous energy. He wore a soiled pair of khaki shorts, forgoing shirts, socks, and shoes, a defense against the myriad fungal threats lurking in the humidity. I could not ascertain whether his boundless energy stemmed from his inherent temperament or the influence of some illicit substance.

Fortuitously, Jenny possessed a hitherto undisclosed skill—proficiency in Portuguese—an invaluable asset in Brazil, a revelation of her remarkable photographic memory that she had kept concealed. However, she chose not to reveal this talent just yet.

With a combination of hand gestures and the captain's limited grasp of English, we negotiated passage to Tabatinga, an arduous six-day journey upstream. The captain offered us a choice for nighttime repose: either to suspend our hammocks from the deck rigging or to share his two available passenger cabins in pairs. We opted for a single cabin for Jenny and three hammocks.

The captain then pointed us toward a nearby shop specializing in hammocks while informing us that he expected two additional passengers. He proposed that we could spend the night on the boat, which we agreed to.

As we settled in, the captain drifted away, searching for a local watering hole. I hoped he had no ulterior motive to report our presence in Manaus to any intelligence agency, leaving us stranded on his timeworn vessel amidst the legendary Amazon River, known for its ravenous piranha.

The following morning, dawn arrived earlier and hotter than we were used to. Two rugged individuals appeared on the dock adjacent to the boat, conversing in Romanian while patiently awaiting the captain's return. Jenny whispered that she comprehended their dialogue but kept her linguistic prowess concealed. Their conversation appeared innocuous, primarily centered on the captain's whereabouts. Eventually, the captain returned, carefully cradling a brown paper bag. Upon boarding, he revealed it contained coffee and pastries, gesturing for the two men to join us. They were still holding their recently purchased hammocks.

I harbored concerns regarding the accommodation of five hammocks on the boat; it seemed a tight fit. The captain engaged the two newcomers in a discussion, primarily conducted in Portuguese, which they appeared not to understand. Jenny whispered that the men merely wished to accompany the captain to his destination and return with him.

As the captain coordinated their needs, we stowed our hammocks in designated compartments along the sides and stern, bearing the label "Life Jackets." I thought life jackets might be impractical in waters infested with piranhas, but I chose not to dwell on the unsettling prospect. I didn't want my companions dwelling on it either, so I kept my thoughts to myself.

With the steam engine roaring to life, we commenced our journey up the river, the bow pounding into the current with rhythmic force. At times, it felt like we were riding a colossal jackhammer while the aged vessel gracefully sliced through the currents at others. The anticipated six-day voyage loomed ahead, offering ample time to decipher the role of the two Romanians in the unfolding mystery. My thoughts also drifted to Wallace— his condition, discoveries, and the ever-enigmatic circumstances enveloping us all.

CHAPTER 39 LANGLEY, VA

Kowalski stood in the doorway of Dunwoody's office. "We've located Wallace's team in Manaus, Brazil," he reported, "though it appears that it might not be the entire team."

"What does that imply?" Dunwoody inquired with a furrowed brow.

"They seem to have split up, possibly to track down both spies simultaneously," Kowalski explained. "We're still working on pinpointing the whereabouts of the other half."

"Do we know whether they're onto Walenski or Karpov?" Dunwoody pressed for information.

"We're still in the dark on that," Kowalski replied.

Dunwoody leaned forward, his tone resolute. "Dispatch a team to Manaus to catch up with that contingent and eliminate them promptly. Attempt to bring one of them back alive. If you find either spy with them, try to bring him back alive."

An hour later, Kowalski, Dunwoody's Assistant Director of Field Operations and chief enforcer, summoned Crystal into his office.

"Crystal, you've demonstrated your unwavering loyalty to Dunwoody, and we're now entrusting you with an expanded role," Kowalski informed her. "You'll be joining a team heading to the Amazon to address a pressing issue there."

"Great," Crystal responded. "Can you give me any details about the target?"

Kowalski shook his head. "I can't disclose anything at this point," he said. "The team leader will brief you upon your arrival in Manaus. Once you're back, provide me with a comprehensive report on the mission's outcome."

"Roger that," Crystal acknowledged, echoing Kowalski's preferred response mode.

As she returned to her office, Crystal couldn't help but wonder about Jake and his team. She fervently hoped that he wasn't the intended target of their operation.

CHAPTER 40 UP THE AMAZON, BRAZIL

The journey up the Amazon was an ordeal, with relentless heat, stifling humidity, and incessant attacks by biting insects. It baffled me how anyone could endure life in such an irritating environment. The constant harassment from mosquitoes, biting flies, fleas, and stinging foliage threatened to overwhelm us were it not for the awe-inspiring beauty surrounding us. The lush vegetation, a vibrant array of flowers in every conceivable color, shape, and size, and a symphony of exotic birdcalls created a sensory experience akin to listening to a captivating piece of classical music.

Initially, the river sprawled wide and swift. As the days passed, it gradually narrowed, branching out so frequently that it became a bewildering maze. Our fellow passengers, non-English speakers or masters of discretion, remained largely silent. They also appeared to struggle with Portuguese, given their evident difficulty comprehending the captain. They tread cautiously when conversing in our presence, relying primarily on hand signals for communication.

At one point, in a broad stretch of the river, the grizzled captain secured the wheel and strolled to the bow. Engaging the two men in conversation, he spoke about an upcoming waterfall, which was when I realized he spoke English. The captain was as crafty as we were. When the two men strained to see the waterfall, I knew they understood English. In less than a second, the captain drew a pistol concealed beneath his shirt and shot both in the back of their heads. One tumbled overboard, and the other he pushed into the water.

"What the hell?" I exclaimed. Jim moved toward his concealed firearm, out of sight of the captain, but I motioned for him to stand down.

"Can't trust anyone in these parts," the captain stated matter-of-factly in English as he holstered his pistol.

"Is there more to this?" I inquired.

"Not at this moment," he replied.

And so, we continued our journey through the murky waters.

After several bends in the river, the captain pointed ahead, revealing a rudimentary dock that I presumed was our destination. We disembarked, watching the captain, who had pledged to wait for our return. Following a solitary native who was anticipating our arrival, we embarked on a winding jungle path. Straining our necks to peer ahead, we expected to encounter a village at any moment where, according to Harold Harper's information, we might find the elusive spy, Nikolai Walenski. We assumed he lived in hiding due to the threats against him, yet we remained ignorant of the reasons or the knowledge he might possess.

As we trekked through the jungle, we engaged in hushed conversations among ourselves, uncertain if our native guide understood English, let alone Portuguese. He didn't appear to be proficient in either.

"Why did the captain kill those men?" Jenny posed the question that weighed on all our minds.

"Were our lives in danger?" Marvin added, echoing our collective curiosity.

"It's possible that someone from an intelligence agency spotted us in Manaus and sent those two to eliminate us once we reached our destination," I speculated. "But why did the captain intervene? Was he safeguarding himself?"

"And if that's the case, Walenski might be in peril too," Jenny pointed out. I couldn't help but concur.

Before long, we arrived at a small village of grass huts. It struck me as odd that we seemed to have entered the village from the rear, with the hut entrances facing away from us. Local natives bustled about, engaged in various primitive activities—preparing food, fashioning utensils, and clothing, or simply sitting in contemplation. Toward the center of the village stood a larger structure, which we presumed to be the tribal leader's dwelling. When we reached its entrance, the native signaled for us to sit around a stone fire pit while he approached the door of the leader's hut. He exchanged words with someone inside in their native tongue before returning to sit beside me and wait with us.

Shortly after that, two women hurried out and vanished from sight. The tribal leader emerged, adorned in leopard skins, a feather cape, and tribal face paint. Yet, one aspect was profoundly unexpected—he was a white man. Not only was he white, but he was also our boat's captain.

A woman brought a rustic stool placing it opposite us. He sat, positioning himself to loom over us—an assertive posture of authority.

"I presume you are Nikolai Walenski, and your native guide took us on a circuitous route to ensure your arrival ahead of us," I stated.

"Yes," he confirmed. "Your fate here will depend heavily on the honesty of your answers to the next few questions."

"We have no reason to deceive you," I replied. "Harold Harper sent us."

"Why didn't he come with you?" he inquired.

"I'm afraid he's deceased," I disclosed.

"Damn," he muttered. "Why then did he send you to me? You've seriously jeopardized my security."

"He believed you possessed vital information that we needed," Marvin explained.

"What I'm about to tell you will place you in grave danger, risking your elimination just as they are trying to eliminate me," Walenski warned. "You should return to Langley, follow your orders, and carry out your assigned tasks. When your conscience begins to trouble you, resign. You'll have a better chance of survival."

"Who is trying to kill you?" I pressed for more information.

He gazed at us for an extended moment. "First, trust no one," he instructed. "Second, locate a French priest named Rodolphe. He has an RFID..."

His words abruptly halted as a commotion erupted behind us, diverting our attention. As we turned to investigate, chaos erupted in the village.

CHAPTER 41 TABATINGA, BRAZIL

Kowalski had assigned Crystal to be part of a team of seven agents tasked with shadowing Jake and his group as they journeyed up the Amazon. However, Crystal was unaware that Jake was one of the targets or the nature of their mission. This Kill Team shared an unwavering loyalty to Dunwoody, reporting exclusively to him and operating in a clandestine manner that remained concealed from those higher up in the CIA. Over time, Crystal had discerned their covert activities and had gradually maneuvered herself into Dunwoody's inner circle.

Shortly after Jake and his team embarked on their journey upriver, the Kill Team set off in a motor launch, maintaining a discreet distance while carefully following Jake's boat along the winding river with its myriad branches and dense overgrowth. Their captain relied primarily on visual cues, tracking the subtle residual waves left by Jake's boat and, in some areas, the smoke emitted by their vessel. Once Jake's boat eventually docked, and the team moved into the jungle, the Kill Team landed at the shoreline adjacent to Jake's location. No one was in sight. They disembarked and furtively advanced on the village where Jake and his team were meeting with Walenski.

The leader of Crystal's team silently instructed everyone to hold fire until he initiated the first shot. Crystal's role was to act as a spotter for the team's sniper. They both lay low on the ground, carefully crawling into a position where they could observe the activities within the village. As she lay beside the sniper, Crystal suddenly spotted Jake and realized he was their intended target. She couldn't bear the thought of her team's sniper shooting at her brother, even if she found herself aligned with the opposition. But she needed to find a way to prevent it.

After settling into position, the sniper began to focus on Jake. Crystal had to act, but she wasn't sure how. Then, an idea struck her. She picked up a small rock and discreetly tossed it behind her, over the sniper's back, ensuring he didn't notice her movement. The rock landed to the sniper's left, producing a faint rustling of leaves—just enough to make the sniper glance toward the sound, checking if someone was approaching from behind. As he turned his head to investigate, he inadvertently exposed his rifle scope to Crystal. Swiftly, she adjusted the horizontal alignment on the top of his scope. He looked back and noticed her nod and give a thumbs-up gesture, signifying readiness. He returned his focus to his target through the scope, oblivious to the subtle modification. When he squeezed the trigger, the bullet missed Jake but found its mark in Walenski, triggering a hail of gunfire and a chaotic scramble in all directions. Jake's team followed him around the chief's hut and into the jungle. Crystal couldn't ascertain if Jake had spotted her.

CHAPTER 42 TABATINGA, BRAZIL

At the sound of the first shot, I heard a "splat," and a red hole appeared in Walenski's forehead. The bullet had gone right past my head to hit him. A red mist flew from the back of his head. Natives scattered, running everywhere -- giving us some cover. We all jumped up, simultaneously pulled our pistols, ran around the chief's hut and dove into the jungle.

"Let's try for the boat," I said. More shots followed. Whoever was shooting at us was not far behind. Walenski had been silenced, but they clearly wanted no witnesses.

We ducked low and ran like hell. At first, we ran helter-skelter through the jungle. Finally, we came upon a path that seemed to head back toward the river. However, as soon as we started down the path, I noticed a fine string across the path. I stopped the others and carefully inspected it -- a booby trap, not built like one of those jungle "mantraps" one saw in old Tarzan movies. No, the string was tied to a Claymore Anti-personnel mine -- think of it as a giant shotgun set to kill anything in a 150-foot-wide semi-circle in front of it. Walenski must have set it. I cautioned them to step over it carefully and to watch carefully for other traps as we moved along the path. We moved as fast as care would allow.

We came upon two more traps before seeing the river. We were about 200 yards east of the dock before we could see the other boat with several men guarding both. It was certain; we would not be going back the way we came. We then heard a loud explosion behind us. Someone had triggered one of the mines. The men guarding the boats didn't leave their posts. Well trained, I thought. We moved away from them, downriver, without being seen. For a short distance, we were able to follow a path but then that path turned back away from the river, and we had to turn to struggling our way through the jungle so we could stay near the river. If we had to get back by walking, we would be a long time in the deep jungle, which was much tougher going but far harder for the others to follow. Marvin told me he heard the shooters speaking English. We had to assume they were CIA or Russians. It wasn't clear why they wanted to kill us other than now we were witnesses to them killing Walenski. I remember commenting to Jenny that I thought I caught a fleeting glance of a woman among the shooters. The mental image momentarily reminded me of my sister, Crystal back in Washington.

After a couple hours, I became comfortable that we had lost our pursuers and figured those that survived the Claymore would return to their boats and use the boats to search along the riverbank. They would know we would have to follow the river to keep from becoming hopelessly lost in the dense jungle that surrounded us. They would scuttle our boat when they departed on theirs. I knew we would be walking a long way, for a long time, through merciless jungle.

I whispered to myself, "Now, this is personal. Nobody shoots at my team and gets away with it." I made a pledge to myself to find the attackers and deal with them.

I couldn't help wondering how they knew where to find us. There was no way they just happened to come upon us. Maybe they discovered where Walenski was and had come after him, unfortunately for us, at the same time we arrived. Or someone had spotted us in Manaus and followed us here. We would never know, but that was my most likely scenario.

That led me to my next question: who had come for us and why? I was also very worried. We were deep in a jungle, hundreds of miles from civilization with not a single soul we could trust between Tabatinga and Manaus. The trip upriver had taken days, but our net rate of speed was quite slow since we were forcing our way against the current. I estimated it would take us at least two to three weeks before we would reach any civilization unless we found another mode of transportation. I realized we were in the greatest danger imaginable -- more than if people were shooting at us. The reason being that we had not the slightest idea about the insects, wild animals, poisonous plants, frogs, snakes, natives, and lord knew what else we would encounter. I found it hard not to let myself panic. But I held myself together for the good of the others.

After Jake and his team disappeared into the jungle, the sniper team leader knew he had screwed up and was in a partial state of shock, staring down at his gun and asking himself unanswerable questions. As the gunfire subsided and their other team members were chasing after Jake's team, the sniper sat dazed.

"I can't believe I missed my target." the sniper said. "What did I do wrong."

"You shot the guy we were supposed to bring back alive," she said.

"You were right here," he said. "Did you see what I did wrong?"

"Not really," she said. "Maybe you jerked the trigger a little rather than squeezing it like you normally would."

"No," he said. "I'm too well trained for that."

He kept staring at his rifle and the scope. Then he looked at the scope closer.

"Hey, the horizontal adjustment is not how I set it," he said.

"I didn't see you bump it," she said. "You must have set it wrong?"

There was a long pause as he ran the possibilities through his head.

"That must have been what happened," he said. Buying into her suggestion. "Man, I've never been that careless. Don't tell Kowalski, will you? We can just say they both moved suddenly at the moment I shot."

"You'll owe me big time if I lie about this for you," she said.

"That's okay with me," he said, scratching his head, as they walked back to their boat to wait for the pursuing team m When the first shot rang out, I heard a wet "splat," and a crimson hole appeared in Walenski's forehead. The bullet had whizzed perilously close to my head before striking its target. A crimson mist sprayed from the back of his head. The native villagers scattered in all directions, lending us a measure of cover. In unison, we sprang to our feet, swiftly drew our pistols, and sprinted around the chief's hut before plunging into the surrounding jungle.

"Let's make a break for the boat," I urged, and more gunshots followed. Whoever was pursuing us wanted no witnesses. With Walenski silenced, they were determined to ensure no one escaped alive.

We crouched low and ran with all our might. Initially, we charged haphazardly through the jungle's undergrowth. Eventually, we stumbled upon a path that appeared to lead back to the river. However, as we began following the trail, I spotted a fine string stretched across it. I halted the others and meticulously examined it, realizing it was a booby trap, albeit unlike the typical jungle "mantraps" depicted in old Tarzan movies. The string was connected to a Claymore Anti-personnel mine—a massive, lethal device designed to unleash a devastating blast in a 150-foot-wide semicircular pattern. Walenski had set it. I warned my companions to step carefully over the trap and remain vigilant for others as we continued along the path, advancing as cautiously as possible.

We encountered two more traps before finally glimpsing the river. We found ourselves approximately 200 yards east of the dock, where several men guarded both boats. There was no doubt we couldn't retrace our steps. An explosion reverberated behind us; someone had triggered one of the mines. Remarkably, the guards at the boats did not abandon their posts, a testament to their training. We moved away from them, following the river downstream, unseen. We managed to follow a path for a brief distance, but it soon veered away from the river, compelling us to hack our way through the relentless jungle growth to stay close to the water's edge. If we had to walk back, we would face an arduous journey through the heart of the unforgiving jungle, which was far more challenging to traverse and exponentially more difficult for our pursuers to navigate. Marvin informed me that he overheard the assailants speaking English. We had to assume they were either CIA operatives or Russians. It remained unclear why they sought to eliminate us, aside from the fact that we were now witnesses to the assassination of Walenski. I briefly mentioned to Jenny that I thought I glimpsed a woman among the attackers, a fleeting image that reminded me of my sister, Crystal, back in Washington.

After a couple of hours, I began to feel confident that we had successfully eluded our pursuers. I suspected those who survived the Claymore explosion would return to their boats and utilize them to search the riverbanks. They were likely to scuttle our boat when they left in theirs. We were facing a long and treacherous journey by foot, deep within the jungle, far from civilization. Our river journey had spanned several days, but our net progress had been slow due to the struggle against the current. It would take us at least two to three weeks before we reached any semblance of civilization, barring the discovery of alternative transportation. We were in a perilous predicament, worse than being shot at, given our complete lack of knowledge regarding the insects, wildlife, poisonous flora, frogs, serpents, indigenous tribes, and other potential threats we might encounter. I fought to keep my panic in check, aware that I needed to remain composed for the sake of the others.

As for our assailants, I couldn't help but ponder how they had pinpointed our location. It seemed improbable that they had stumbled upon us by chance. Perhaps they had learned of Walenski's whereabouts and had arrived to apprehend him simultaneously with our arrival. Alternatively, someone might have observed us in Manaus and trailed us here. We would never know, but my working theory leaned toward the latter scenario. That led me to the crucial question: who had come after us, and what was their motive? I was deeply concerned about our situation, stranded in the heart of a jungle hundreds of miles from civilization, with no one we could trust between Tabatinga and Manaus. Our journey upriver had been arduous, and our current predicament was fraught with uncertainties. She smiled because she now had something on the sniper that might come in handy sometime in the future. The spy business was like that, collecting "chips" to be cashed in later when the need arises. If only she knew where Jake was now.

CHAPTER 43 IN THE AMAZON JUNGLE

We pressed on through the dense jungle until darkness descended upon us. Our journey was frequently impeded by streams and marshy terrain, forcing us to venture deep into the interior before circling back to the river's vicinity. Occasionally, we fashioned makeshift rafts from old logs and vines to cross river branches. Thankfully, I had the foresight to carry a small compass on a cord around my neck, a habit I had picked up from my days with Outward Bound. With the onset of night, we veered further inland to find a patch of dry ground where we could rest.

While Jenny had a cigarette lighter, we dared not kindle a fire despite the evening chill. A fire would have provided warmth and deterred nocturnal predators like the black jaguars that prowled the surrounding jungle. As they say, we reentered the food chain. Even our drinking water presented a dilemma with no food and uncertainty about edible plants. The river water teemed with bacteria and amoebas, making it more perilous to drink than not, but our bodies could only endure three to seven days without water, and ten at the most. Jim had a pocketknife, which he used to fashion a small spear. I doubted its effectiveness against a formidable adversary like a large cat, but it might give him time to draw his gun. We knew we would have to employ our firearms if confronted during the night, necessitating vigilant watch duty in pitch darkness—an unnerving task. We managed to fashion crude cups from leaves and positioned them beneath the drip lines of a couple of trees to collect dew overnight.

Come morning, we savored the meager sips of water we had gathered and resumed our quest to follow the closest river branch to the east. After a day's trek, the terrain grew increasingly hilly, and we stumbled upon a rickety bridge spanning a wide gorge filled with rocks and rushing water. The bridge consisted of woven vines with floorboards fashioned from slender kindling, no more than two inches in diameter. I ventured about ten feet onto it to test its stability and found it shaky but capable of bearing our weight. As we prepared to cross, I noticed that Marvin was perspiring profusely.

"Are you feeling all right?" I inquired.

"I'm not sick if that's what you mean," Marvin replied.

Jenny regarded Marvin with her head cocked at an odd angle.

"I think he might be afraid of heights," she suggested.

Marvin lowered his head and nodded slowly. Jim stepped closer to Marvin, and I thought he was about to offer some comforting gesture.

"This calls for a technique I've used with unruly mules," Jim declared before delivering a solid punch to Marvin's jaw.

Marvin collapsed instantly, unconscious. Jim hoisted him over his shoulders and cautiously carried him across the bridge. Midway across, Marvin regained consciousness, glanced both ways and promptly fainted again. On the opposite side, after Jim gently set him down, Marvin awoke again.

"Don't you ever do that again," he growled. Jenny and I arrived at the scene.

"You'd have felt guilty if we had backtracked for miles," Jim quipped with a grin.

"All right, it's over," I interjected. "Let's keep moving."

"It wasn't all that bad," Marvin remarked to Jenny. "Except my jaw is going to be sore."

We continued for another two days until we unexpectedly encountered well-worn paths, signaling the proximity of a village. We exercised even greater caution than before. We couldn't predict whether the natives were in contact with their western neighbors, possibly sympathetic or colluding with them, or naturally hostile to outsiders traveling alone. Furthermore, we needed to consider their heightened sensitivity to the sounds and scents of the jungle. Thankfully, the wind was in our favor, carrying our scent away from the village. We managed to crawl close enough to observe the village without rousing alarm. The locals appeared unfazed, going about their daily tasks, which included repairing their thatch and mud huts, grinding grains or seeds, and shuttling fish and fruits collected from dugout canoes along the shoreline. I signaled for us to retreat to the west and await the cover of darkness. Despite the relentless insect attacks, we remained clear of their paths and attempted to banish thoughts of hunger and thirst. We were growing weary, and our strength waned.

We were blessed with a moonless sky that night, which made silent jungle navigation particularly challenging. Our movements startled a flock of birds or monkeys in the treetops, but fortunately, they weren't howler monkeys whose cacophonous cries might have alerted the natives. We reached the dugout canoes and discovered paddles stowed inside. Jim and Jenny shared one, while Marvin and I occupied the other. Jim and Jenny exhibited greater coordination in their paddling, whereas Marvin and I struggled to synchronize our efforts. However, with practice, we gradually improved our technique. Jim and Jenny often paddled backward to close the gaps that would open between our canoes. Eventually, we realized that the river's current was strong enough that by positioning our dugouts alongside each other and gripping one another's vessels, we could traverse as a single unit, paddling only on the outer edges to maintain our course.

The river channel widened at one point, and we heard a troubling sound—the putt-putt of a steam-driven boat approaching from behind. It was well past midnight, and the moon was now visible, albeit shrouded by clouds. We steered our canoes toward the riverbank and crouched low to avoid casting silhouettes against the vegetation. In the distance, we discerned a spotlight projecting ahead of the boat. While we couldn't identify any occupants in the darkness, we could hear muffled voices. The boat was heading downstream with a sense of purpose. Perhaps they intended to intercept us in Manaus.

As the boat drew nearer, we endeavored to remain as still as possible, hugging the shore tightly and gripping overhanging branches to anchor ourselves against the current. We even pulled down some vegetation to create a makeshift cover. The boat emerged from the misty night with its feeble single light illuminating its path ahead. It passed us by in a sluggish manner. They appeared intent on traveling downstream, perhaps planning to lie in wait for us in Manaus.

Once they had moved beyond our position, we resumed our downstream journey. We paddled intermittently, often allowing the current to carry us to conserve our energy. I couldn't help but wonder about Abigail and the others in Alaska during our desperate struggle for survival.

CHAPTER 44 THE VATICAN

Luis Carlotti entered Cardinal Mendolini's dimly lit office and gently closed the intricately carved wooden door, creating a soft thud. The Cardinal, engrossed in his work, didn't lift his gaze from the desk before him. It was as if he possessed eyes on the top of his balding head.

"What do you want?" he inquired in a low, commanding tone.

"We need a stroll in the lush garden," Carlotti suggested.

The Cardinal rose from his seat after placing his signature on the parchment before him. Without uttering a word, he followed Carlotti as they ventured into the serene garden, bathed in the golden hues of the fading sun.

Once surrounded by the tranquility of nature, the Cardinal turned to face Carlotti, his eyes piercing like a falcon's. "Well?" he demanded impatiently.

"We have successfully neutralized half of the team responsible for the turmoil in Bucharest," Carlotti began.

The Cardinal arched a questioning eyebrow. "And where did you locate them?" he inquired; his curiosity piqued.

"In the remote Aleutian Islands, of all places," Carlotti disclosed. "They stumbled upon Karpov."

A glimmer of hope sparked in the Cardinal's eyes. "Have we apprehended him? Did he lead us to Walenski?" he inquired eagerly.

Carlotti hesitated, choosing his words carefully. "Not precisely," he replied.

"What exactly do you mean?" the Cardinal pressed impatiently. "Speak plainly, man."

"Regrettably, Walenski was not found in that vicinity," Carlotti confessed. "And, well, Karpov... he took his own life."

The Cardinal fell silent for a moment, his thoughts racing. "Before or after that rogue team made contact with him?" he probed further.

"Afterward, I'm afraid," Carlotti admitted.

A stern look crossed the Cardinal's face. "You should indeed be..."

"Be what?" Carlotti inquired, his voice quivering under the Cardinal's stern gaze.

"Afraid," the Cardinal stated firmly. Carlotti involuntarily recoiled.

"When you mentioned 'neutralized,' you meant they were killed, correct?" the Cardinal clarified, his tone unyielding.

Carlotti hesitated once more. "Well," he began tentatively.

The Cardinal's patience wore thin. "Can you not speak plainly?" he demanded.

"The captain of the ship, who led the team we hired to track Karpov and Walenski, abandoned them when they fled," Carlotti finally admitted.

"Is there any possibility they survived?" the Cardinal inquired; his voice laced with frustration.

"We believe it to be unlikely," Carlotti responded.

"But you are not certain," the Cardinal deduced. "You had better prepare for the possibility of their survival and resume your search. Pray they do not reappear. And what of the other half of the team?"

"They emerged in Brazil, embarking on a journey up the winding Amazon River," Carlotti revealed. "We managed to corner them in a remote village, where they encountered Walenski. They had just initiated a conversation with him when one of our operatives eliminated Walenski."

The Cardinal's eyes widened in disbelief. "Eliminated Walenski? We needed him alive! Are you fools? How do you expect us to recover the stolen plans, taken by Karpov and Walenski, if they are both deceased? Did you at least successfully eliminate that faction of the rogue CIA team?"

"They fled into the impenetrable jungle," Carlotti explained. "The wilderness is vast, leaving them hundreds of miles from civilization, surrounded by perilous flora and fauna. It is highly improbable that they will ever resurface. They are effectively dead. However, we failed to locate the stolen plans."

"Pray they do not resurface," Mendolini declared sternly. "There is far too much uncertainty in how you have conducted these operations, and incompetence runs rampant in this organization despite the substantial compensation provided. As you leave, send Archbishop Santanio to me."

Carlotti retreated from the Cardinal's presence, his brow damp with perspiration. If either faction of those teams reemerged, his fate would be sealed. There were three potential scenarios, any one of which could lead to his demise. If both or either faction surfaced, he would face certain death. Only the slim possibility that neither would resurface offered him a fleeting glimmer of hope. Carlotti returned to his office, determined to intensify the global search for either half of the rogue teams.

CHAPTER 45 DOWN THE AMAZON, MANAUS BRAZIL

After discreetly circumventing several quaint villages under the cloak of night, we gradually encountered more and more people. A sense of relief washed over us, suggesting that we had successfully distanced ourselves from the relentless pursuers. It took a week and a half of arduous trekking, but we finally arrived at a small town that offered us a reprieve. We indulged in savory street food there, replenished our supplies with bottled water, and secured seats on a dilapidated, weathered bus bound for Manaus. In a moment of resourcefulness, Marvin secured our passage with his cherished Rolex, as our financial resources remained limited. We were acutely aware that if we reached Manaus, we would need to exercise utmost vigilance against any lingering agents tracking our every move until we could reach Paris.

The bus we boarded was a creaking relic adorned with a clutter of luggage tied haphazardly to its roof. There were as many chickens and goats on board as passengers.

At one point during the journey, the bus came to an abrupt halt, intercepted by an army patrol. The soldiers briefly scanned the passengers, but our over ten days of immersion in the jungle made our clothes tattered and our skin darkened by a combination of sun, sweat, and dirt. We blended seamlessly with our fellow passengers, evading their scrutiny. Exhausted, we seized the opportunity to catch some much-needed sleep during the remainder of the ride.

Arriving in Manaus without further interruptions, we proceeded with caution. We went to the bank where we had concealed our bags and meager funds. Subsequently, we located a modest one-star hotel, booking two rooms – one for Jenny and the other for Marvin, Jim, and myself. After cleansing ourselves of the grime accumulated during our ordeal, I dispatched Jim to secure additional sustenance. Once he returned, we convened in my room, eager to discuss our next course of action.

"We must identify someone we can place our trust in. It's evident that someone was pursuing Walenski, and perhaps all of us. Someone knew we had gone to meet him," Jenny observed.

Jim chimed in, "What about Jerry? Can we rely on him?"

"I believe so, but only him," I replied cautiously. "I intend to call him to gauge his knowledge."

I sought privacy within the hotel's lobby, utilizing a phone booth to ensure no one eavesdropped on my conversation. I was mindful that if the call were somehow traced, it would require considerable effort to locate us in this obscure hotel, let alone our rooms. It took several attempts to reach Jerry, and I refrained from disclosing my identity.

"Hello, old friend," I greeted him, maintaining my discretion.

Jerry, equally cautious, responded, "Don't reveal your location. What do you require?"

I continued, "The contact we went to meet has been eliminated."

Jerry's response intrigued me. "I've heard they dispatched a retrieval team, not an elimination squad."

"Can you provide insight into the broader context? There appears to be something significant in play, but it remains uncertain," I inquired.

"I concur, but I lack complete information at this juncture," Jerry admitted. "My superior seems perturbed by something, and I suspect it pertains to you."

"Have you had any communication with my second-in-command?" I probed.

Jerry's response was disquieting. "Negative. I find it disconcerting that you are unaware of their whereabouts."

"I fervently hope our paths will intersect soon," I remarked.

Jerry shared his apprehensions. "There's a conspicuous gap in my knowledge. Forces are working to keep me in the dark. Even my typically loyal contacts have fallen silent. Here's my proposition – call me again in an hour. I intend to delve deeper, utilizing a resource I've yet to tap."

We exchanged goodbyes, and I rejoined the team outside, proposing a brief stroll to a nearby park. It would serve as an observation point, allowing us to monitor the hotel's entrance. We remained vigilant, wary of any potential pursuit triggered by my conversation with Jerry or any surveillance on our call. One hour later, with no signs of suspicious activity, I returned to the hotel lobby alone while the team remained poised in the park, ready to intervene if needed.

As I approached the lobby's phone, it began to ring. I answered, and it was Jerry on the line.

"Here's what I've uncovered," he began. "My immediate superior, whom I won't name, authorized a 'departure party' for you and your team – no doubt about it. Have you encountered them yet?"

I responded with caution, "You could say that."

"Why would they want you 'departed'?" Jerry pressed.

"I believe it's linked to what we're trying to unearth," I explained. "It's evident they want to safeguard something they're desperate to keep hidden. I wish I knew what that something is."

Jerry proceeded, "I found no trace of your partner's whereabouts. When and where did you last see her?"

"We parted ways on our journey here," I disclosed. "She embarked on a quest to locate another source, but I'm uncertain of her destination, capiche?"

"I comprehend," Jerry acknowledged. "I'll keep my ear to the ground. Should you require further assistance in the interim, don't hesitate to reach out."

"We're adequately equipped for now," I affirmed. "I must end the call. Au revoir."

By concluding with the French term for goodbye, I subtly alluded to our ultimate destination – Paris. I returned to the team outside and relayed the information I had gleaned from Jerry.

"It's clear that our organization is determined to eliminate us," I declared solemnly. "Yet, the motive remains elusive. My trust in Jerry is wavering. We must be closing in on something of tremendous importance. Vigilance is our only defense. We'll continue following the trail until we can corner our elusive prey."

"Are we transforming into bloodhounds now?" Marvin quipped.

With a sly grin, I retorted, "How do you say 'bloodhounds' in French?"

"Limiers," Jenny offered.

"You're a fascinating bunch," Marvin commented.

"In your endearing way, you are too," Jenny replied.

"Let's not linger," I urged. "Our journey leads us to Gay Paris, where we hope the remainder of our team awaits. Unbeknownst to us, we are walking into the lion's den."

CHAPTER 46 LANGLEY, VA

Crystal was keenly aware of Jake's extensive wilderness survival training, but even that couldn't overshadow the daunting expanse of the Amazon jungle, where the odds of his survival appeared tenuous at best. Following the ill-fated mission in the Amazon, the team's leader and sniper faced demotion upon their return to Langley. In a surprising turn of events, Crystal was promoted and entrusted with the mission to confirm the team's whereabouts that had vanished into the treacherous jungle.

Jerome Wallace, Jake's supervisor, had recuperated from his injuries and was discharged after several more weeks. Crystal visited Wallace, her true motives concealed, to extract any information he might possess regarding Jake and his missing comrades. Wallace remained oblivious to her identity as Jake's sister and the directive from Dunwoody. A seasoned and cautious spy, Wallace opted to supply her with misleading details. He informed her that he had lost contact with the team and was actively working on reestablishing communication. Deep-seated concern gnawed at Crystal for Jake's safety and the potential repercussions of his demise. Nevertheless, she concealed her anxieties, placing her faith in Jake's formidable survival skills.

Upon departing from Jerome's office, Crystal returned to her workspace. She had implemented a tracking system on the bank accounts belonging to Jake's team members, expecting some financial activity if they were to resurface. Regrettably, her investigation yielded no trace of money transfers, intensifying her apprehension.

Subsequently, Crystal went to Dunwoody's office and delivered her report: the missing team had yet to reemerge. Convinced that their fate likely involved perishing in the unforgiving jungle, Dunwoody promptly dismissed her as he prepared to meet with Director Rogers.

CHAPTER 47 LANGLEY, VA

Dunwoody stood resolutely before Director Rogers' imposing desk, ready to face the stern inquiry that had been inevitable.

"Why haven't you located Rhodes and his team yet?" Rogers' inquiry pierced the silence of the room.

"They've managed to go off the grid," Dunwoody responded with a tinge of frustration.

Dunwoody understood that he needed to bear the brunt of the criticism, at least for now. He recognized that his ascension to Roger's position in the organization was only a matter of time. Yet, he remained mindful of Cardinal Mendolini's directive to exercise patience and continued to play his part in this elaborate charade. He relished the prospect of soon settling scores with Rogers.

Rogers' rhetorical question hung in the air: "Can we get any more incompetent? What are you going to do?"

Inwardly, Dunwoody couldn't help but savor the knowledge that Rogers was entirely unaware of his ulterior motives. A fleeting urge to smile flitted across Dunwoody's face but was swiftly stifled.

"We've deployed agents worldwide to watch for them," Dunwoody replied. "Additionally, we've issued a fabricated Red Notice through Interpol. They're actively assisting in the search and will notify us when they surface."

Rogers probed further, questioning the legitimacy of the charges against Rhodes' team.

"What charge did you fabricate for that Interpol notice? You're well aware that they don't entertain political charges."

"We've framed it differently," Dunwoody revealed. "We've made it a concrete commercial charge—alleged theft of valuable corporate patent information that hadn't yet been officially filed. Interpol has already disseminated the alert to their global offices."

Rogers, however, remained unimpressed. "It sounds rather amateurish to me," he commented. "Update me instantly if you receive any information about them."

With a nod of acknowledgment, Dunwoody pivoted on his heel and exited the office, leaving behind a director who still believed Rhodes' team to be a solitary, ill-equipped entity with no clear objectives. Yet, he couldn't help but wonder what was percolating in the mind of Cardinal Mendolini, observing Dunwoody's repeated failures to halt Jake Rhodes.

CHAPTER 48 THE VATICAN

In the Vatican, Santanio entered Mendolini's office, where the Cardinal's face was flushed with anger, resembling a powder keg about to detonate.

"You summoned me, Your Eminence?" Santanio inquired.

Mendolini nodded, his ire palpable. "I trust you'll understand if we engage in a more discreet conversation without venturing to the garden," he said, speaking indirectly.

Santanio assented with a nod.

"Direct our discreet operative to initiate production and assembly," Mendolini declared. "We shall furnish them with further instructions later, specifying when and where to deliver their output for deployment. It is time for us to set in motion the snowball that will gather mass and momentum beyond the comprehension of all but a select few."

"As you command, Your Eminence," Santanio acknowledged before turning to depart.

Mendolini, however, sensed a trace of doubt and inquired, "Do you harbor reservations?"

"It is not my place to question decisions made by those chosen by the Pope, considered holier than I," Santanio responded.

"But if the Pope sought your counsel, would you concur?" Mendolini probed.

"As with many aspects of life," Santanio began, "if the ultimate goal is just, are not the means also considered just?"

"When the objective is to spread the word of God," Mendolini asserted, "all actions are deemed just."

"Amen," Santanio concurred as he exited the office to carry out the instructions. "Before I go, I must inform you that Dunwoody has reported that half of the CIA team has resurfaced in Manaus, Brazil."

Mendolini's face registered a momentary flicker of hope. "And they've been dealt with, I presume?"

Santanio hesitated briefly. "No, Your Eminence," he admitted. "We suspect they may have adopted new identities and vanished once more. Their whereabouts remain unknown."

Mendolini shook his head and gestured for Santanio to depart.

Santanio could not shake off his concerns. The whereabouts of the other half of Jake's team remained a mystery. He clung to the hope that, at this juncture in the plan's execution, he was indispensable, though that was his only lifeline for survival.

CHAPTER 49 PARIS

Utilizing our alternate identities, we successfully navigated Manaus airport's security, avoiding suspicious scrutiny. After a layover in Brussels, Belgium, our flight eventually touched down at the Paris airport.

Customs proved uneventful, and we promptly hailed a taxi to our prearranged meeting place, a hotel where we hoped to rendezvous with Abigail and her team. My sense of security had heightened in the bustling city until we reached our destination. During the taxi ride from the airport, we engaged in mundane conversation, posing as typical American businesspeople searching for franchise opportunities – our fabricated cover stories. The cab driver displayed no interest in our uninteresting dialogue, a reaction we had hoped to elicit.

Having encountered several weeks of delays, I couldn't help but worry that Abigail and her team might have been compromised during our absence. However, upon reaching the hotel, we discovered Abigail, and her team safely ensconced in one of the larger reserved rooms, calmly lounging.

Initially, everyone spoke simultaneously, eager to exchange stories. I was inquisitive about Abigail's experiences and whether she had encountered adversaries as we had. It was heartening to see that all members of her team had survived. I had faith that if anyone could navigate the challenges and bring them through unscathed, it was Abigail. None of us genuinely comprehended the gravity of the dangers we were entangled with.

Amid the excited chatter, Abigail was bursting to share her news with me. "I believe I spotted one of Dunwoody's operatives in the customs area at the airport when we arrived," she divulged. "I don't think he noticed us, but I can't be certain. We managed to speak with Karpov, but he's no longer alive."

"Karpov's deceased?" Jake inquired. "I'm eager to hear more about that, but let's not dally. Whoever pursued the two agents we visited is likely hot on our trail now. We must keep moving."

"Yet, we remain clueless about the 'why,'" Abigail mused.

As we busily packed our belongings and strategized our move to another hotel, we exchanged accounts of our respective team's experiences. Abigail recounted what Karpov had told her: "Find the priest Rodolphe and the message he carries." In return, I conveyed our findings: "The message is in the form of an RFID."

"What's an RFID?" Jim inquired.

"It stands for Radio Frequency Identifier chip," Max explained. "It's a data storage device that can only be accessed using a scanner. In this instance, someone likely encoded a message on it, though it would need to be concise as these chips have limited capacity."

"First, we must locate Rodolphe," I asserted. "It's time to apply those research skills we honed back at Langley while maintaining a low profile."

Our situation had reached a critical juncture, compelling us to delve into the heart of the unfolding mystery, remain vigilant, and relocate to another discreet hotel.

CHAPTER 50 THE VATICAN

Strolling through the garden, Mendolini and Santanio delved into the status of their intricate plans.

"So, Archbishop, what's our latest status?" Mendolini inquired.

"Except for that rogue CIA team still eluding us, everything remains on schedule," Santanio reported. "Organizationally, we are fully prepared to execute your orders to remove Demidov, Cheng, and Rogers. Khachenski, Kuang, and Dunwoody are in their positions, ready to step in and assume control. The moment you give the green light, you will effectively wield authority over the world's intelligence agencies. Our people, including their Secret Service teams, are strategically placed around them, poised to eliminate their presidents and the key figures in their respective military hierarchies. We are primed to seize control of the administrative branches of the superpowers."

Mendolini nodded in agreement.

"And the Pope is still unaware of your plan, correct?" Santanio inquired.

"I'll inform him when the timing is impeccable," Mendolini replied. "This has been one of the primary reasons why maintaining absolute secrecy about our plans has been paramount. Even at this late stage, we must ensure that no one gains knowledge of our intentions. The train is hurtling down the tracks now, and a minor obstacle could derail the entire operation if you catch my drift. It is crucial that you begin consolidating your resources and tightening your controls. And deal with that troublesome rogue team immediately! That's all for now."

Santanio couldn't help but wonder whether Mendolini harbored ambitions regarding the Pope's position. If Santanio were privy to the extent of the Rogue Team's knowledge, his apprehensions would be even more pronounced than they already were.

CHAPTER 51 LANGLEY, VA

Kowalski had returned to Dunwoody's office, pacing back and forth with an air of urgency.

"You won't believe our stroke of luck," Kowalski began. "One of our operatives spotted three rogue team members disembarking from a flight at Orly Airport."

Dunwoody leaned forward; his interest piqued. "Which ones? The ones from the Aleutians or the Amazon?"

"The ones from the Aleutians, or at least they arrived on a flight from Alaska," Kowalski confirmed. "They hopped into a taxi, but we managed to trace their movements through the taxi company to a small hotel in the city."

"Is the hotel under surveillance?" Dunwoody inquired.

"Yes, it is. Once any team members venture out, we'll tail them, and at the first inconspicuous opportunity, we'll eliminate them," Kowalski explained.

"Excellent," Dunwoody responded. "I want you to dispatch Crystal and a team to Paris to clean up this mess. Add one of your more discreet operatives to her team to be extra cautious. He can monitor the others and report back without her knowledge. We're not taking any chances at this stage."

Kowalski nodded in agreement. "One more thing, sir. We intercepted a weak radio signal from the vicinity of the team's hotel. Do we have any listening devices in place?"

Dunwoody frowned. "Not that I'm aware of. Get me the frequency, and I'll set up monitoring to decipher its purpose. Pass the information to Cindy."

"Should I inform Mendolini about our actions?" Kowalski asked.

Dunwoody considered for a moment. "Not just yet. Let's wait until we've cleaned up the situation."

Little did they know that the Vatican had already sensed something was amiss.

CHAPTER 52 THE VATICAN

Archbishop Santanio strolled through the garden alongside Cardinal Mendolini, their conversation hushed and urgent.

"Both the CIA and SVR have deployed teams to Paris," Archbishop Santanio disclosed. "They've been tight-lipped about their objectives, but we suspect they've located at least part of the rogue CIA team."

Cardinal Mendolini nodded thoughtfully. "Summon Carlotti and his team into action," he ordered. "In case the CIA or SVR fumble their operation, I want a contingency plan. We must ensure that this thorn is extracted. And, before we make any moves, ascertain why they've converged in Paris. Our paramount objective is to recover the stolen copy of our plans and seal this leak."

"I'll mobilize Carlotti's squad without delay," Santanio affirmed, turning on his heel to head back indoors. They knew the whereabouts of the rogue team, but the contents of their knowledge and purpose in Paris remained a pressing enigma.

CHAPTER 53 PARIS

I led the team to the American Library at #10, Rue du General Camou. With the assistance of a helpful librarian, we managed to uncover articles from local English-language newspapers that were of interest to the English-speaking community in Paris. Utilizing annual indexes compiled by the newspaper publishers, we tracked down articles related to Rodolphe, who we discovered had been a celebrated spy tragically killed a few years earlier.

Further research revealed Rodolphe's notoriety as a French espionage figure who had met his demise alongside a small, loyal cadre of compatriots. Their exploits had unveiled an unnamed yet formidable conspiracy, leading to fabricated charges of espionage and fratricide among spies. We found mentions of two other spies implicated with Rodolphe, who had managed to evade capture, and we now realized that these two spies were the individuals we had encountered in the Amazon and the Aleutians.

"It seems," I mused to the team, "that the message hidden within the RFID suggests the involvement of rogue agents within their intelligence agencies." The conspiracy had been skillfully concealed following Rodolphe's demise. What struck us as peculiar was the absence of any reported cause of his death. I couldn't help but wonder if he had met his end at the hands of individuals he had trusted. Amid our research, we also uncovered the name and location of the cemetery where Rodolphe had been laid to rest.

Convinced that we had gathered sufficient information, I addressed the team, saying, "It's time to retrieve that RFID and unravel the mystery behind this conspiracy."

Jim asked, "Do you think the RFID is merely buried with him?"

"I would wager that since it wasn't discovered during his burial, someone may have implanted a microchip within Rodolphe himself," I speculated.

Marvin interjected with another concern, "But even if we locate his body, how will we find the RFID if it's concealed on or within his body?"

Jim added, "And even if we find it, how do we decipher its contents?"

Abigail contributed, "In the event, it's internally placed, where on his body do you think we should look? Neck, arm, leg, chest?"

Jenny thoughtfully replied, "It's unlikely to be in any of those places. I'd say the loosest skin would be on the side of his torso, beneath his arms."

Jim contemplated the logistics, stating, "We'll need to search for a puncture wound or scar unless we're prepared to examine his entire body systematically."

I clarified our next step, "The newspaper mentioned his burial in a mausoleum and provided details about the cemetery. Breaking into a mausoleum should be more manageable than exhuming a coffin. We know where he rests; let's proceed."

Abigail hesitantly said, "You mean like sneaking into a cemetery in the middle of the night? I'm not particularly fond of that idea."

I couldn't help but notice Abigail's vulnerability revealed by her fear of entering a cemetery at night. Peculiarly, I felt relieved that she had displayed a hint of weakness.

"How about this," I proposed, "I'll handle that part with my half of the team while you and your team focus on locating a radio scanner capable of reading the RFID's contents."

Abigail agreed, her response quick and decisive, "Deal." It was as if she wanted to secure the agreement before I could reconsider.

I wasn't thrilled about the prospect of grave robbing, but it was a necessary step in our mission.

CHAPTER 54 MONTMARTRE CEMETERY, PARIS

The night it enveloped us in an inky blackness akin to the depths of an unlit forest on a moonless night. Shrouded by Earth's shadow, the moon remained concealed until dawn due to its New Moon phase. Marvin, Jenny, Jim, and I silently moved along parallel paths amidst the cemetery's tombstones. Recognizing the darkness we would encounter, we forgone the need for all-black attire, opting for simple sweatpants and shirts. As we navigated, our vigilant eyes scanned for watchmen, grave robbers, late-night lovers, or adventurous teenagers—anyone who could inadvertently stumble upon us and disrupt our mission. Our objective was a small mausoleum in section 24, near the final resting place of Fernando Sor, an early 19th-century composer and guitarist.

To bypass the cemetery's main entrance, sealed at night by a massive iron gate, we scaled a short wall crowned with wrought-iron fencing along Rue Etex. This tactical move shortened our traverse through about two-thirds of the cemetery's width, avoiding the entire length. Armed with a map of the cemetery, procured from the library, I carried a small flashlight concealed under a red cellophane sheet to prevent blinding myself with its white light. Red light's wavelength transitions eyes from rods to cones more smoothly than white light, preventing temporary blindness—a critical advantage. According to our research, the mausoleum bore the name "Famille de

Roi," which matched Rodolphe's family name. Our team came prepared with the requisite tools, and we discreetly entered the mausoleum within minutes.

Inside, we discovered imposing stone vaults, each adorned with nameplates. We promptly located Rodolphe's burial vault and, with concerted effort, managed to shift the hefty marble lid. Within, we encountered a desiccated body—leathery skin stretched over deteriorating bones. As a leader, I believed in being willing to undertake even the most undesirable tasks, so I retrieved a box cutter I had brought to extract the RFID. However, I faced uncertainty about its exact location. I scrutinized the area we believed to be most promising: the flesh on the side of the chest beneath the arm. Inspecting the right side yielded no hints—no telltale impressions or protrusions on the skin. The vault's placement along the mausoleum's outer wall, with the body's head to my left, limited my access to the left side of the body.

"Jim and Marvin, lend me a hand in turning this skeleton toward me," I directed.

"Must we?" Marvin questioned.

"Summon your courage, Marvin," Jim encouraged.

Together, the two men and I gently rotated the body while Jenny watched at the door. At that moment, I spotted a slight ridge along the fourth rib. Employing the cutter, I sliced through the leathery skin, like cutting a sturdy leather belt—resilient and resistant. After diligent effort, I successfully retrieved the device and examined it closely. My expectations had been set for something the size of a grain of rice, but this was a small capsule measuring half an inch in length and as thick as a large nail. To ensure I didn't lose it or accidentally drop it on our way back to the hotel, I cautiously placed it inside one of the hotel's letter envelopes, designated for this purpose, and secured it in one of my pants pockets with a buttoned flap. We carefully restored the crypt's lid and reached the door. Judging by Jenny's expression, she was more than eager to depart.

We discreetly closed the mausoleum's outer door behind us and ventured toward Rue Etex. Near the street, we encountered minimal ambient light. Given the late hour, nearby houses lay shrouded in darkness, and sporadic streetlights were dim from infrequent maintenance. I believed we had eluded any potential danger. However, out of the corner of my eye, I caught a glint of faint light reflecting off a metallic object. I froze, raising my fist high to signal the others to halt. Shifting my palms downward and moving them in an up-and-down motion indicated for them to crouch down. In an instant, gunshots erupted— numerous rounds originating from our forward right and behind us. The assailants had orchestrated an ambush, strategically positioning themselves to converge fire upon us without endangering one another. I instinctively touched the cross hanging from a chain around my neck—the one bestowed upon me by Crystal as a token of good fortune. Our only recourse was to fight through one of the sides, as we had the wall beside us and gunfire emerging from two angles, offering no avenue for retreat. I signaled for us to advance toward the hail of gunfire from our right, targeting half of their force to force the others to cease firing.

"If we engage with half their assailants, it will deter the remaining half from shooting," I declared in a firm but subdued voice. "Fire at the muzzle flashes. Now, run!"

Considering our rigorous training, the team followed my lead, firing precisely. Soon, we had four attackers incapacitated, creating an opening for our escape. As I passed by one of the fallen foes, I noticed the assailant was clad entirely in black, his face obscured by darkened camouflage. It was a coordinated attack against us. Time was of the essence, so there was no opportunity to investigate their pockets or weaponry to ascertain who had dispatched them to eliminate us. We sprinted eastward, then clambered over the wall. The approaching wail of police sirens led me to believe our assailants wouldn't pursue us; instead, they would focus on eliminating evidence before facing law enforcement's scrutiny. I had faith that they wouldn't want to be exposed.

We maintained a brisk yet inconspicuous pace as if we were local joggers out for an evening run, gradually putting distance between ourselves and the cemetery. Since we had left our tools behind at the mausoleum, we could move swiftly without arousing suspicion from the residents we encountered. Thankfully, our gloved hands meant the tools bore no fingerprints. The route from Montmartre led downhill to our hotel, and we jogged without excessive exertion.

Eventually, after we had covered sufficient distance and executed several turns, we slowed to a walk. Jenny turned her attention to a pressing question. "Once we ascertain what's on the chip, whom can we trust with this information beyond our team?"

"That's an excellent question," I acknowledged. "Let's postpone worrying about that until we unveil the chip's contents."

Upon our return to the hotel and settling into my room, I noticed an oddity in Jim's behavior. "Did you get hit?" I inquired.

Jim inspected his arm and belatedly noticed that he was bleeding. "I suppose I did," he admitted. "With all the adrenaline, I didn't even notice it. It's starting to hurt quite a bit now that I'm aware."

"We need to seek medical attention," Marvin suggested.

I approached to examine the wound more closely, tearing open Jim's shirt and using the torn fabric to cleanse the coagulated blood, inadvertently causing the damage to bleed once more. "It's a shallow wound, and the bullet passed through," I assessed. "I believe we can manage the treatment here. We'll require some basic first aid supplies."

Jenny quickly offered a solution, "I spotted a pharmacy on the next block. I bet I can find a standard first aid kit there."

"Why don't you see what you can procure while keeping a low profile?" I suggested.

Meanwhile, Abigail, Vincenzo, and Max having explored the possibility of acquiring an RFID reader at an electronics store, discovered that such establishments were scarce in Paris. Following a visit to a hardware store to procure essential burglary tools, they located a source for veterinary supplies, reasoning that it would be less secure and off the beaten path. Regrettably, the nearest source was situated within the Ministry of Agriculture, offering no promise of minimal security. Nonetheless, their advantage lay in the sprawling complex of buildings, making it challenging for police to pinpoint any break-in alarm. They selected a building, infiltrated it, retrieved an RFID reader, and departed without incident. Armed with knowledge gained from her library research, Abigail recognized the reader as a handheld device similar in size to a portable telephone.

Upon regrouping at the hotel, we crowded into my room. I initiated a discussion regarding the ambush. "How did they know we would be in that cemetery tonight?" I wondered aloud.

Abigail asked, "Who were the individuals that attacked you?"

"They exhibited professionalism and organization," I stated. "Uniform attire, all armed with Kalashnikovs."

"That doesn't narrow it down much," Marvin remarked. "Why didn't Abigail's team encounter an ambush like ours?"

"Have all of you been vigilant about ensuring no one is trailing you?" I inquired.

Each team member nodded or verbally affirmed their diligence.

"I'm not convinced it's safe to remain in our rooms tonight," I expressed my concerns. "Jenny, head down to the lobby and secure the Presidential suite, which is located at the end of this floor. We'll leave our belongings in our rooms but bring only our firearms. Wear something comfortable to sleep in but leave your pajamas to create the appearance that we've suddenly departed. Don't forget to bring the RFID chip and the scanner. Call it paranoia on my part."

"Should I bring my laptop?" Marvin asked.

"No, it's too risky for tonight," I advised. "Ensure it has a robust password and encrypt critical files separately, so no sensitive information can be accessed even if it's taken. Additionally, affix a sticker or piece of tape to the case to determine if it has been tampered with. Let's make it appear like we departed in haste, leaving behind our watches, jewelry, and all other personal effects."

Jenny retrieved cosmetic tape from her purse and handed it to Marvin, who nodded in agreement.

"Set up some indicator to tell if someone entered your room," Abigail suggested. "For instance, you could close a strand of your hair in the door as you exit."

Jenny promptly departed and returned with the room key. Subsequently, we dispersed to our respective rooms. I removed my watch, the wooden cross bestowed upon me by my sister, and my belt, placing them on the bathroom sink with the cross partially atop the watch—a simple method to determine if either had been moved.

Within the Presidential suite, we adopted the appearance of a slumber party, each occupying their designated space—bed, sofa, chair, or sprawled out on the carpet. Abigail, Max, and I gathered at the desk while Marvin worked diligently to decode the information retrieved from the RFID. Marvin reported his findings, "It seems to be shaping up as a series of global positioning coordinates. There's also a reference to a book by Arthur Rimbaud titled 'A Season in Hell.'"

"I've heard of that book," Jenny interjected. "It's scarce, with copies only found in major libraries and no longer accessible to the general public. It would be in archives or 'The Stacks,' as some libraries refer to their restricted areas. Gaining access will be challenging. But why do we need it?"

"The man was a spy," I reasoned. "The encoded chip was intended to lead us there for a reason. We must pursue this lead, especially since at least four people have given their lives for it."

Abigail addressed an essential issue, "Let's say we acquire compelling evidence. Whom do we take it to? Who can we trust? Our trainer, Jerry? Certainly not his superior. How high does this conspiracy reach? Do we attempt to reach the President or trust a Senator?"

"We'll have to go as high as we can," I asserted. "We'll need to convince Jeremy and Dunwoody to accompany us or take all three of them to meet with the President's Chief of Staff—without disclosing the reason. I doubt they'll comply with such a request. Moreover, even if they believe us, can we safely reach that meeting without being targeted by whoever is pursuing us? We'll need to wait until we have more information. For now, let's try to get some rest. We'll take shifts listening at our door. I'll take the first shift, followed alphabetically by first name."

"Sounds like a plan," Vincenzo approved.

As I sat by the door, maintaining vigilance and listening intently, I couldn't help but ponder who was pursuing us, the motive behind their actions, and what lay ahead in this perilous journey.

CHAPTER 55 LANGLEY, VA

Kowalski walked into Dunwoody's office.

"Our team ambushed that Rogue Team in a Paris cemetery last night, but against all odds they escaped," he said. "I am astounded that they gave us the slip again. These are no fools. We sent a man to watch the hotel room they used last night, but I don't think they will go back. If they do, we'll get them there."

"Communications has been listening to a radio signal from that area," Dunwoody asked. "It has an identification code and is coming from a miniature device we assigned a couple of years ago, to an agent named Madansky. Do you know him?"

"Yes," Kowalski said. "He's one of mine. Why?"

"Find out from him what happened to the device," Dunwoody said. "I want to know how it got from him to that CIA team. Try not to let on why we want to know."

"Is the signal moving?" Kowalski asked.

"Yes," Dunwoody said. "It appears to move with the team. We picked it up at that hotel and monitored it as it moved to that Paris cemetery. However, it transmits a weak and broad signal, so we must be close to the team, and it can be hard to pinpoint its exact location."

"If we can confirm they are at the hotel, we can wipe them out now" Kowalski said.

"I want to learn why they are in Paris," Dunwoody said. "At this point, I want them captured alive so I can find out exactly what they know and who they've told. Send men to watch the other hotels in the area, the airports, and the train stations in case they don't return to that hotel, I don't know why they are in Paris, but I have a gut feeling they haven't gone far. Keep a man in place to watch their old rooms but let our entire network in France know to keep an eye out for them in

Kowalski entered Dunwoody's office; concern etched on his face.

"Our team tried to ambush the Rogue Team in a Paris cemetery last night, but they somehow managed to slip away," he reported. "I can't believe they outsmarted us again. These guys are not amateurs. We did place a man to monitor the hotel room they used last night, but I doubt they'll return. If they do, we might catch them there."

Dunwoody leaned forward; his brow furrowed. "Our communications intercepted a radio signal in that vicinity," he informed Kowalski. "It's transmitting from a miniature device we assigned to an agent named Madansky a couple of years ago. Do you know him?"

Kowalski nodded. "Yes, he's one of my agents. Why do you ask?"

"Find out from Madansky what happened to the device," Dunwoody instructed. "I want to understand how it ended up with that CIA team. Try to keep our real motives concealed."

Kowalski inquired, "Is the signal currently on the move?"

Dunwoody confirmed, "Yes, it appears to be moving with the team. We picked it up at that hotel and tracked it as it shifted to the Paris cemetery. However, the signal is weak and widespread, making it challenging to pinpoint their exact location."

Kowalski contemplated their options. "If we can confirm they've returned to the hotel, we can take them out immediately."

Dunwoody shook his head. "I'm keen on discovering why they're in Paris. At this juncture, I want them captured alive so we can extract information regarding their knowledge and contacts. Deploy our personnel to monitor other nearby hotels, airports, and train stations so we will find them if they don't return to the hotel. I don't know why they are in Paris, but I have a hunch they haven't strayed too far. Maintain surveillance on their previous hotel rooms and inform our entire network in France to be on the lookout for them in all the usual spots."

Kowalski nodded, understanding the gravity of the situation, and left Dunwoody's office to execute the orders.

CHAPTER 56 PARIS

The following morning, I carefully cracked open the door to our suite and peered out, spotting a solitary figure lurking in a dim alcove of the hallway, keeping a watchful eye on our abandoned rooms. After gently closing the door, I whispered to Abigail, instructing her to strip down to her underwear and stroll down the corridor, passing by the observer and pausing by the elevator. With a sly smile, Abigail complied with my request, slipping into the hallway unnoticed by the man down the hall. Seizing the opportunity, I slipped out of the suite, and while the man remained fixated on Abigail's path down the hall, I stealthily approached him and rendered him unconscious with a swift blow from the butt of my pistol. Abigail and I swiftly dragged him back into the suite, securing him with restraints and a blindfold.

"Let's retrieve our belongings from our rooms and make our exit," I suggested. "Our destination is the Bibliothèque Nationale de France."

We swiftly gathered our possessions from our rooms, noticing that the hair indicators we'd placed in the door jambs had vanished. The intruders had been professionals, leaving no traces and maintaining the illusion that we were unaware of being under surveillance.

I strapped on my belt and wristwatch and tucked my cherished cross and pistol into my knapsack.

As we boarded the elevator to depart, I pressed the button for the basement rather than the lobby. "We're making our exit through the back," I explained. "It's likely they have operatives in the lobby."

Navigating through the basement, we ascended a staircase to access the back alley without drawing attention. We reached the National Library near the Louvre, securing special permission to access the Archives section. Inside an ancient, priceless book indicated by the RFID, we discovered a cavity carved out in the middle, housing a floppy disk. Defacing such a rare book struck me as sacrilegious, suggesting that Rodolphe had resorted to an unconventional hiding place to evade detection. I retrieved the disk and carried it to a table where Marvin had already set up his laptop. We began deciphering its contents, revealing a horrifying, meticulously detailed plan.

"These plans are beyond appalling," I remarked. "It's difficult to fathom anyone harboring such malevolent intentions. We must validate its authenticity through a secondary source before taking action based on this plan, which carries monumental consequences."

Abigail questioned, "Is there anyone we can trust to assist us based on this information?"

"We'll need to deliberate on that carefully," I responded. "This implies that we shouldn't trust anyone within our Organization back at Langley."

Marvin added, "Achieving this level of infiltration into major spy agencies by external forces would require extensive planning, organization, and a strong presence throughout the organization. It would also demand time, absolute secrecy, and immense patience."

Jim expressed his concerns, "Employing such a heinous weapon is not just irresponsible; it's downright evil."

Jenny pondered, "But why? What could be the motive behind this?"

"At the very least, the plan reveals the location of the carbon Nano-tube manufacturing facility," I stated. "We can head to the factory in Rome, secure samples, and if they align with the plan's specifications, it will serve as the confirmation we need."

Abigail emphasized, "That's just the beginning of what we'll have to do to address this crisis. We're facing an immense challenge with no one we can trust for assistance."

Jim voiced concerns about transportation: "How do we get to Rome without being spotted? They could be monitoring all transportation hubs."

"I assumed that planes, buses, and trains would be watched," I admitted. "So, we'll need a large van or a couple of inconspicuous cars."

Marvin raised a practical point, "But how do we afford rental vehicles and train tickets? Jenny has funds, but not here in Europe, right?"

Jenny clarified, "I do have resources here, too, but there's a risk they might be tracked. The good news is that I have a sister with a different last name and equal financial means. I can contact her, and she can set everything up as if she's coming to Paris to collect the van, embark on a European tour, and eventually ship it back to the U.S. after her trip. Any van dealership would gladly accept cash and facilitate the arrangements. I'll ensure she orchestrates it so I can pick up the van under the pretense of delivering it to her upon her arrival, although she won't be leaving the U.S. This should make it untraceable."

We proceeded to arrange for the van, and within a day, it was ready. Opting for a hostel for the night, we believed it would be less likely to be under surveillance. Setting out for the first train stop south of Paris, Lyon, and leaving the van behind, we thought this approach minimized our chances of being detected. It also seemed reasonable to assume that our pursuers, aware of our arrival by plane, would anticipate we depart the same way or by train, reducing their focus on train stations outside the city. It was a calculated risk.

Upon our arrival in Lyon, we took precautions, spreading out and maintaining low profiles, adopting our baseball coach's hand signals for communication. Touching our left elbow indicated the sighting of someone suspicious, while touching our hair was the all-clear signal. Folding a hand into a fist meant regrouping, and raising an open hand above the head signaled a need to scatter quickly and seek cover.

We boarded the train without incident, sitting separately within the same carriage, some facing forward and others backward to maintain a vantage point for spotting approaching individuals.

CHAPTER 57 LANGLEY, VA

Kowalski had Madansky seated in his office. Madansky, a tall and outspoken agent, wore a frown as he listened to Kowalski's questions.

"Two years ago, we issued you a small transmitter for tracking an individual's movements," Kowalski inquired. "Do you recall what happened to it?"

Madansky quipped, "Am I in trouble for overdue fines like at the library?"

Kowalski retorted, "Don't be a wise guy. You've probably never set foot inside a library. Where's the device now?"

Madansky explained, "I planted it on one of our agents, Crystal Johnson, to monitor her and ensure her trustworthiness, just as you instructed."

Kowalski recollected, "Ah, yes, I remember now. Do you think she still has it?"

Madansky shrugged, "How should I know? We stopped tracking her once she was cleared. I never retrieved the bug."

Kowalski nodded and said, "All right, that's enough for now."

Madansky left Kowalski's office with a dismissive shrug. Kowalski, on the other hand, was left puzzled by the revelation. He wondered if Crystal was still wearing the cross and if she was currently in Paris. He had his doubts.

He headed to Dunwoody's office and found his superior standing behind his desk, slamming the phone in frustration.

Dunwoody immediately briefed him, saying, "The signal from that transmitting bug just appeared in Rome. You need to get there urgently and neutralize that team. No excuses. Get it done. They're getting uncomfortably close."

CHAPTER 58 ROME

Concerned that the train to Rome and the arriving station might be under surveillance by authorities and determined not to attract any unwanted attention as we entered Italy, we adopted a strategy of dispersing throughout the passenger cars and altering our disguises. Additionally, we synchronized our departure from the train to minimize our visibility. Some of us disembarked quickly, blending into the crowd, while others lingered behind until most passengers had left the train. Maintaining a low profile as individuals rather than as a group was paramount to our safety.

Marvin, seated next to me, had diligently researched our options with the train conductor. He had discovered another obscure hotel on the Left Bank of Rome where we could lay low, at least temporarily. He had also obtained information about the carbon Nanotube factory's address, where the mysterious weapons described in the plans were purportedly being manufactured. Though we didn't fully comprehend the nature of these weapons, the name "Nano" suggested they were small, but the extent of their miniaturization remained a mystery.

The urgency of our mission was apparent. We needed to break into the carbon Nanotube plant that night, hoping to obtain critical information before our pursuers caught wind of our presence. We huddled in the hotel room to hash out the details of our operation.

Before departing for the factory, I retrieved my gun and cross from my backpack and secured them in their customary positions on my person. We left the hotel discreetly, dispersing in small groups.

Upon arriving at the factory, we discovered that it wasn't just a carbon Nanotube facility but also a bio-laboratory. This revelation hinted at a grim outcome. Fortunately, the lab's security was lax, allowing us to time the guard patrols and slip inside through a side entrance between rounds. Abigail, Max, and Vincenzo positioned themselves at critical intersections within the building to maintain silent communication as we navigated the premises.

As we proceeded through the building with small flashlights, we passed offices with windows that revealed most of their materials were locked in secure vaults. My group reached the main office and began scouring their files. We encountered a locked file drawer, but Marvin skillfully picked the lock, granting us access to the documents we sought.

What we uncovered shed light on the rest of the sinister plan. The project involved manufacturing a substantial quantity of carbon Nanotubes, which would be filled with a newly discovered strain of time-release Anthrax. Anti-Muslim sentiments were evident among the notes within the file. The most shocking revelation was that the orders had originated from Archbishop Carlos Santanio's office.

Including such incriminating information in a manufacturing file was a careless blunder of the clandestine operation. It provided valuable insight, suggesting that either egos or an extensive grip on the local authorities had led to such recklessness. We stashed the pertinent files into our backpacks.

Just as we finished gathering our findings, a whispered message came from the hallway, alerting us to approaching men dressed in black. I ordered everyone into a nearby stairwell to reach the roof. As they entered the building, the assailants would proceed cautiously, first inspecting the lower levels, giving us a chance to escape through the rooftop.

Upon reaching the roof, we realized the factory was interconnected with adjacent buildings. We could traverse from roof to roof across multiple structures, provided we acted swiftly and evaded the pursuit team, depending on its size.

We reached the last building and descended the internal stairwell to assess whether the exit was clear. Once confirmed, we exited and sprinted through the streets, several blocks away and around multiple corners, until we reached a point where we could reduce our pace to a walk.

I signaled everyone to stop when I believed we had achieved a safe distance.

"They tracked us again," I muttered to myself. "How do they know our every move? There must be a tracking device on us. Check your clothing and backpacks."

We emptied our pockets and knapsacks, meticulously inspecting every seam, cuff, and tag. However, we found nothing suspicious. I glanced down at the cross I was wearing, a gift from my sister, and a sudden intuition struck me.

"It can't be," I said, removing the cross and placing it on a low concrete wall. "I hate to do this, but I have to know." I took out my pistol, turned it butt-first, and struck the cross forcefully. The wood splintered slightly, revealing a small electronic chip. I examined it closely in the dim light of a nearby streetlamp. "Damn," I muttered. I pounded the chip relentlessly until it was rendered inoperative, then buried it in the dirt with my bare hands. I collected the pieces of the cross and put them in my pocket. "Let's move."

We dispersed again in small groups, creating distance from our last known location, where the enemy could have tracked us.

As we walked, I continued to speak aloud, grappling with the disturbing realization that my sister might be connected to those attempting to kill us. I couldn't comprehend how she could betray me and our country after raising me and earning my trust throughout my life.

"I'm sorry, but the evidence is hard to ignore," Abigail offered sympathetically.

"That's how they located us in the Amazon, in Paris, and now here," I realized aloud. "It must have been something we left behind in our hotel rooms because, if it were on us when we moved into the suite, they would have known we were there."

"You're making a valid point," Abigail agreed.

I continued to voice my mounting questions and doubts, reflecting on various instances when my sister's behavior had seemed suspicious. The puzzle pieces began to fall into place, revealing a dark and troubling connection.

Upon our return to the hotel, we couldn't take any chances. Although we no longer had a tracking device divulging our location, we switched hotels again. In our new accommodations, we registered in pairs and groups of three, securing four separate rooms.

Once we had settled into our new hotel, we convened to discuss the conspiracy we had uncovered and our next steps. The files from the laboratory were extensive, and it would take most of the night to sift through all the information.

We uncovered damning evidence related to the production of Anthrax and the development of an antidote in large quantities. The files suggested that the conspirators were prepared for millions of innocent casualties—a chilling prospect. However, the nature of the delivery mechanism for the infected carbon Nanotubes remained a mystery, with the source of this component seemingly separate. To thwart this elaborate scheme, we needed to ascertain the delivery mechanism, understand the motivations behind the mass extermination, pinpoint the timeline, and identify potential allies who could assist us in stopping it.

CHAPTER 59 THE VATICAN

The following morning, we gathered in my room. Abigail and I had spent most of the night poring over the files. We caught a few hours of sleep in the early morning, waking up as the others started stirring.

Once we were alert, I began sharing our findings. "It appears that the Vatican is at the heart of this conspiracy," I stated. "Archbishop Santanio seems to be the key figure, acting as the sole contractor for the facility. However, he mentions needing clearance from a higher authority, but he doesn't disclose the identity of this superior in the notes we found."

"It's almost inconceivable that the Vatican could be involved in such a plot, but the evidence is compelling," Abigail remarked.

"At this point, we can only speculate about their true motives, but the potential consequences are undoubtedly catastrophic. We'll have to unravel their true intentions as we work to stop them," I added.

"Their plan, while disturbingly straightforward, reflects a certain level of genius and, simultaneously, sheer madness," I continued. "We need to locate and halt the mastermind behind this."

Abigail stood up and voiced her thoughts. "Considering their infiltration of major security agencies and their ability to manipulate insiders who appear loyal, along with their plan to target large Muslim populations globally, it suggests they may be striving for some form of New World Order, not unlike what Hitler aimed for."

"All signs point to the Vatican as the epicenter of this conspiracy," I said. "Still, we lack definitive proof. It's conceivable that this entire file could be the product of a delusional mind or an abandoned plan."

"Given the extensive materials found in that factory, it's unlikely this was a mere fantasy," Max said.

"Before we attempt any action or involve others, we need to penetrate the Vatican and verify, from within, the authenticity of this plan's origin within their walls," I proposed.

"But we also need to determine who we can trust to share this information with," Abigail added.

Marvin suggested a solution. "I have an idea. I can dismantle the RFID reader to create a few transmitting devices. Vincenzo could blend in with visiting clergy groups with his priestly disguise and knowledge of Latin. He might plant a bug in or around Santanio's office."

"If we can make more bugs, then we should. We can't be certain of all the conspirators," I agreed.

Marvin confirmed, "I have materials for three transmitters, and I'll need to acquire a transistor radio and take some parts from the hotel's phones."

Vincenzo added, "I can dress as a priest, and Jenny can join me disguised as a nun. It'll enhance the deception when I purchase the nun's habits."

"That's a good plan," Vincenzo said. "I believe it will add credibility to our deception. We should be cautious and realistic. We can't expect to uncover more than Santanio's involvement."

As we planned our next steps, we remained unaware of the tightening net around us.

CHAPTER 60 THE VATICAN

Santanio walked into the Cardinal's office, patiently waiting for Swiss Guard officer Tito Galli to exit. As Galli left, the Cardinal addressed him sternly, "Your security measures are far too lax. Rectify the situation promptly, or you'll face the consequences, understand?"

"Yes, sir," Galli replied.

Once Galli was out of earshot, Santanio wasted no time and urgently spoke, "We need to have an immediate discussion."

"This one time, we can talk here," Mendolini agreed. "All the adjacent offices are vacant today. Everyone is attending the local conclave except us; we have more pressing matters."

"None of our teams in Paris managed to neutralize that rogue CIA unit," Santanio explained. "Not only did they escape in Paris, but now they've resurfaced in Rome, and the two halves of the team have reunited."

"Remarkable, given that half of them disembarked in the middle of the Bering Sea during winter while the others traversed hundreds of miles in the Amazon jungle," Mendolini commented.

"It appears they also infiltrated the factory in Rome," Santanio continued. "We aren't certain about the duration of their presence, but there are indications they may have located a copy of the factory plans."

"Our Vatican team was present as well, and they failed to eliminate them?" the Cardinal inquired with frustration. "We're plagued by incompetence. This cannot persist."

"We acted as soon as we received word from Dunwoody," Santanio replied. "It seems the CIA had some method of tracking them."

"Order them to use that tracking method to locate and eliminate them immediately," the Cardinal demanded.

"They've lost the signal," Santanio revealed. "It's likely the team found and disabled the tracking device."

"We must alert the factory and fortify their security," the Cardinal insisted. "We cannot afford them returning, infiltrating, and halting production. That plant poses our most significant vulnerability. Any disruption there would set our mission back for years. Focus solely on this."

Santanio promptly exited the room.

The following day, Archbishop Santanio strolled through the garden with Cardinal Mendolini.

"Our situation has gone from bad to worse," Santanio admitted. "We've confirmed that they obtained a copy of our plans. On a positive note, the assembly process is well underway, and they won't be able to stop that. However, they may now know who is orchestrating it."

"They've acquired a set of our plans, which is troubling enough," Mendolini responded. "But how on earth could they ascertain the mastermind behind the operation?"

"Carlotti discovered that our production personnel retained more information in their files than they should have," Santanio explained.

"As soon as the production is complete, we must eliminate the plant manager for his negligence," Mendolini declared. "Reducing potential witnesses is always prudent."

"Agreed, once the assembly is done," Santanio acknowledged.

"Our peril is severe," Mendolini emphasized. "Locate and terminate that rogue team immediately. It's not just your highest priority; at this moment, it's your sole focus. Is that clear?"

"Yes, sir," Santanio replied, bowing and stepping back.

CHAPTER 61 THE VATICAN

Santanio entered the Cardinal's office, patiently biding his time until Swiss Guard officer Tito Galli had exited. As Galli departed, the Cardinal addressed him sternly, "Your security measures are grossly inadequate. Remediate the situation promptly, or you will face severe consequences. Do you understand?"

"Yes, sir," Galli responded.

Once Galli had moved out of earshot, Santanio wasted no time and spoke urgently, "We need an immediate discussion."

"This is the one instance where we can converse here," Mendolini concurred. "All the adjacent offices are currently vacant. Everyone else is attending the local conclave, leaving us with more pressing matters."

"None of our teams in Paris neutralized that rogue CIA unit," Santanio explained. "Not only did they evade capture in Paris, but now they have reemerged in Rome, and the two halves of the team have rejoined."

"Remarkable, considering that half of them disembarked in the middle of the Bering Sea during winter while the others trekked hundreds of miles through the Amazon jungle," Mendolini commented.

"It appears they also managed to infiltrate the factory in Rome," Santanio continued. "We are uncertain about the duration of their presence, but there are indications that they may have obtained a copy of the factory plans."

"Our Vatican team was present as well, and they failed to eliminate them?" the Cardinal inquired with frustration. "We are plagued by incompetence. This incompetence cannot be allowed to persist."

"We took action as soon as we received word from Dunwoody," Santanio replied. "It seems the CIA possessed a means of tracking them."

"Instruct them to employ that tracking method to locate and eliminate the rogue team immediately," the Cardinal demanded.

"They have lost the tracking signal," Santanio revealed. "It is highly likely that the team discovered and disabled the tracking device."

"We must promptly alert the factory and reinforce their security," the Cardinal insisted. "We cannot afford the rogue team to return, infiltrate, and disrupt production. That plant is our most glaring vulnerability. Any disruption there would set our mission back by years. Concentrate solely on this matter."

Santanio swiftly exited the room.

The following day, Archbishop Santanio walked through the garden with Cardinal Mendolini.

"Our situation has deteriorated from bad to worse," Santanio confessed. "We have confirmed that they acquired a copy of our plans. On a more positive note, the assembly process is well underway, and they will not be able to impede that. Nevertheless, they may now possess knowledge of the orchestrator behind it."

"They have obtained a set of our plans, which is concerning," Mendolini responded. "But how could they discern the mastermind behind this operation?"

"Carlotti discovered that our production personnel retained more information in their files than they should have," Santanio explained.

"As soon as the production is complete, we must eliminate the plant manager for his negligence," Mendolini declared. "Minimizing potential witnesses is always prudent."

"Agreed, once the assembly is finalized," Santanio concurred.

"Our peril is dire," Mendolini stressed. "Locate and eliminate that rogue team immediately. It is not just your highest priority; at this moment, it is your sole focus. Is that clear?"

"Yes, sir," Santanio replied, bowing and stepping back.

CHAPTER 62 THE VATICAN

Vincenzo and Jenny found themselves in a quandary inside the Vatican, unsure of their next move. Armed only with the name of the Cardinal from the factory records, Cardinal Santanio, they proceeded cautiously, aware of their limited knowledge about his role within the Vatican. Vincenzo started by asking a passing priest for directions to Cardinal Santanio's office. The priest, also a visitor to the Vatican, couldn't provide precise directions but pointed them down a hallway toward the offices and suggested they inquire further there.

Approaching the office area, they noticed signs indicating it was restricted to authorized personnel only. As they pondered their next steps, a burly man emerged from the office area's open arched entrance and confronted them with an intimidating tone, asking, "May I help you?" Despite the brevity of his words, his demeanor put them on edge.

Playing it off, Vincenzo feigned ignorance and replied, "Could you please direct us to the Library?" The gruff-looking man hastily provided directions leading in the opposite direction. Vincenzo awkwardly maneuvered the wheelchair around in the narrow corridor while the impatient man moved on without waiting for them to leave the area. As soon as he disappeared around a corner, Vincenzo halted and backed the wheelchair up to the open archway, providing them a discreet vantage point to observe and eavesdrop on. A sign next to the door read,

"Vatican Secretary of State," and they could see a series of spacious offices through the open door. Voices resonated from one of the offices.

"You are fortunate that Cardinal Ludwig is in Brazil, Archbishop Santanio, or I would have your head," a voice exclaimed.

"But, Cardinal Mendolini, this is a matter of utmost urgency," another voice argued. "The factory is fully prepared."

"Not here, you imbecile," Cardinal Mendolini snapped. "Follow me."

Vincenzo held one of the miniature bugging devices in his hand while Jenny carried the other two. As the Cardinal and Archbishop hurried past them, Vincenzo deftly slipped a bug into the Archbishop's robe pocket. The bug was minuscule, making it unlikely for him to notice even if he reached into his pocket.

After loitering in the nearby hallway, Vincenzo and Jenny caught a lucky break. With the Cardinal and Archbishop temporarily absent from the office area and only Mendolini's assistant remaining, the assistant decided to step outside for a smoke break. On his way to a balcony designated for smoking, he even asked Vincenzo to whistle if he spotted the Cardinal's return. Out on the balcony, the assistant unwittingly turned away from Vincenzo and Jenny as he enjoyed the panoramic view of the city. This lapse allowed Vincenzo to discreetly slip into the offices and plant two bugs. He positioned one in the Cardinal's larger office, assuming it was his superior's office, and the other in Santanio's office. While in the larger office, Vincenzo managed to identify it as the workspace of Cardinal Mendolini from documents scattered on the desk. He also seized the opportunity to acquire the assistant's identification key card, reasoning that if its disappearance went unnoticed for some time, it might grant them access to the Vatican after hours in case of future necessity.

CHAPTER 63 OUTSIDE THE VATICAN

As we eavesdropped on the bug's transmission, we could hear Cardinal Mendolini conversing with Archbishop Santanio. We assumed that Vincenzo and Jenny had managed to leave the office area before Mendolini and Santanio returned. The Cardinal's voice carried as he berated his assistant for abandoning his post within the office area. While scolding his assistant, an unexpected visitor arrived, presumably a messenger. We overheard him addressing the Cardinal with crucial information.

"I was dispatched to inform you that our Rome network has reported a suspicious group of Americans staying at Hotel San Aventus," the messenger conveyed. "This is the complete message Il Signore Dunwoody requested me to deliver. Do you have any response you'd like me to convey?"

"No, thank you," Mendolini replied. "You may leave."

The revelation left Marvin and I stunned.

"Holy crap," I exclaimed. "Dunwoody is betraying us. Clearly, we can't trust him with what we've discovered."

We continued to listen to the conversation unfold.

Mendolini declared, "That must be the Rogue team we've been tracking. Fetch Carlotti and instruct him to assemble a team immediately to confront them."

After some papers were shuffled, we heard Santiago return with Carlos Carlotti.

"Your Excellency, this is Crystal Johnson, our most skilled team leader," Carlotti introduced her. "She can lead a team to eliminate that Rogue team."

"She's Dunwoody's top operative," Santiago added.

"What are you waiting for?" Mendolini urged. "Provide her with the best operatives you have and dispatch them to Hotel San Aventus immediately to neutralize those Americans."

"Crystal, go fetch Kowalski and a dozen of our most capable operatives and handle this immediately," Carlotti instructed. Crystal must have immediately acted because we didn't hear any further mention of her.

"I hope you know what you're doing," the Cardinal commented to Carlotti.

The conversation ended, and all that remained was the sound of papers shuffling. Upon hearing that my sister had been dispatched to eliminate my team and me, I was left in utter disbelief. It was startling to learn that she was a CIA agent affiliated with Dunwoody. Yet, the most inconceivable and devastating realization was that my sister would be willing to take my life. At that moment, our bug ceased to transmit.

"They might have moved out of range," Marvin suggested.

Little did we know that Crystal herself might soon be in jeopardy.

CHAPTER 64 BEHIND THE VATICAN

An hour later, Carlotti found himself walking in the garden alongside Mendolini, the weight of unsettling revelations bearing down on them.

"Our informant at the hotel revealed that the team leader is Jake Rhodes. We conducted an extensive CIA background check on him. Dunwoody knew he was the leader, but he didn't know this. It turns out an older sister raised him," Carlotti disclosed.

Mendolini raised an eyebrow. "And why is that relevant?"

"Her name is Crystal Johnson," Carlotti replied. "Does that ring a bell?"

Mendolini's expression shifted to one of realization. "The lead agent of the team we just dispatched to eliminate Rhodes?" he asked. "So, you're telling me Dunwoody didn't know they were related? That Jake Rhodes and Crystal Johnson are siblings?"

"He claims he did not know of it," Carlotti confirmed. "It never surfaced during Rhodes' background check because he had reported that both of his parents were deceased, and she used her married name on all official documents."

"This is even more serious than I had anticipated," Mendolini admitted, his tone fraught with concern. "Her motivation for infiltrating us may have stemmed from a desire to uncover the truth about her parents' deaths and their connection to our organization. Now, she not only possesses intimate knowledge of our plans but also operates from the heart of our operation. She poses a greater threat than any other risk we face. She must be eliminated immediately. Send our most elite and loyal squad of Swiss Guards to the same hotel and instruct them to eliminate everyone present, including her and her team. Spare no one."

"I'd lead the squad myself, but it's safer for me to remain here in case they attempt to target you," Carlotti explained. "I'll dispatch Tito Galli; he has experience from the old days in Bucharest, and Marco Mazza, who has previously executed such operations for me."

Mendolini's voice carried a note of regret as he responded, "You should have sent them from the beginning."

CHAPTER 65 ROME BANK

Abigail and her team took turns tailing the man who had left the Vatican. He walked a considerable distance, occasionally glancing behind him to ensure he wasn't being followed. Eventually, he met up with Dunwoody in front of a large bank. Dunwoody had been patiently waiting next to an armored car. As soon as they met, Dunwoody escorted him into the bank. While Jim and Marvin discreetly observed from the bank's front window, Abigail entered, attempting to blend in as an ordinary customer.

She relied on the hope that Dunwoody wouldn't recognize her, given her disguise of a wig and sunglasses. She saw him hand over a check and sign a document from her vantage point. Although she couldn't discern the paper's content, she overheard the bank manager addressing him as Mr. Madansky. Then, two bank guards emerged from the area containing the open vault door, pushing a substantial cart loaded with canvas sacks labeled "reales" and "dinars," the currencies of various Middle Eastern countries, including Iran, Saudi Arabia, and Syria. Some of the sacks were even labeled as U.S. dollars. The guards proceeded to load the sacks into the back of the armored car. Abigail and her team were left baffled, wondering what the Vatican intended to purchase with such an extensive amount of currency.

As the currency was being loaded into the armored truck, Abigail and her team quickly realized that they needed to follow the truck. They promptly hailed a taxi and piled into it. The taxi driver was instructed to wait as they kept a close watch. Once the truck was fully loaded, Madansky sat in the passenger seat, adamant about accompanying the driver to its destination. Meanwhile, Dunwoody departed on foot, heading back towards the Vatican. Abigail and her team trailed the truck in the taxi, leading them to the exact factory from which they had obtained the plans.

Upon arriving at the factory, Abigail could see that the security had been significantly bolstered. The added security meant that the Vatican's plan was beginning to unfold, and the danger was becoming increasingly evident to all of them. Once they comprehended the gravity of the situation, they knew they had to contact Jake immediately. They had discerned how the Anthrax would be dispersed: through the currency. It was imperative to halt the process before the factory could contaminate the money and send it on its way. However, they were acutely aware that they lacked the manpower to attack the factory in its fortified state. They needed assistance—considerable assistance. So, they hastily returned to the hotel to rendezvous with Jake and the rest of the team. And yet, the identity of the Vatican's mastermind behind this heinous act and the motive remained shrouded in mystery.

CHAPTER 66 OUTSIDE THE VATICAN

Marvin and I sat in a rental car parked along one side of the Vatican, strategically positioned to observe the windows of the offices that Vincenzo and Jenny had bugged. We anxiously listened for any transmissions. Eventually, Vincenzo and Jenny returned, joining us in the car, and miraculously, the bug was again operational.

At a pivotal moment, we overheard Mendolini utter, "We are on the brink of launching our New World Order under the guidance and leadership of His Holiness the Pope. When he witnesses our achievements, he will be compelled to appoint me as his successor when the time comes." Their sinister plan involved leveraging Christianity to exert control over major governments worldwide. These revelations confirmed that Mendolini was the mastermind behind the conspiracy, the proverbial head of the snake.

Yet, the most alarming revelation came when we heard them dispatching my sister and her team to our hotel. It was evident that they not only knew our hotel's location but, more heart-wrenching for me, Crystal was one of them. I didn't have the luxury of dwelling on my own emotions. Since we had yet to witness their departure from the Vatican, we knew they would emerge fully assembled and armed soon. Avoiding a return to the hotel was not an option; we were compelled to leave.

With Abigail, Jim, and Max on a separate mission, we hastened back to the hotel. Our paramount objective was to ensure that they weren't caught off guard. We departed while the conversations were still in progress, knowing we might return later to gather further intelligence, provided the bugs remained undetected and we could avoid their lethal "Kill Team." My thoughts were consumed by the impending encounter with my sister and her team at the hotel. Little did we know that another team was following closely behind hers.

CHAPTER 67 THE VATICAN

Jenny, Vincenzo, Marvin, and I raced back to the hotel, hoping to run into Abigail, Max, and Jim to avoid a potential confrontation with my sister's team. Our main concern was keeping our comrades from being ambushed. Fortunately, we reached the hotel before the Vatican squad and our fellow agents returned. Arriving in time allowed us to set up an ambush of our own in the hotel's rear courtyard.

The hotel featured an interior courtyard at the back, a two-story space measuring about 75 feet square, open to the sky. A second-story open balcony corridor encircled it. The walkway had a solid stone three-foot high wall serving as a railing all around it. This short, protective wall provided both cover and ideal shooting angles—head-on from their arrival and left side. By selecting only two sides in the shape of an "L," we minimized the risk of crossfire among our team members. I left Marvin on watch to alert us when the Vatican team arrived, so we had enough time to take our positions before Abigail, Max, and Jim returned.

As the Vatican team, led by Crystal, entered the hotel and approached the courtyard, Crystal wisely halted them, recognizing the potential for an ambush. After scanning the area and failing to spot us, hidden behind the solid wall railing while crouched down, she ordered her team to disperse and advance cautiously into the courtyard. As they entered, it became apparent that we were there, and they opened fire. During the exchange of gunfire, I noticed that Crystal was deliberately not firing at any of us. Realizing this, I urgently instructed my team not to shoot their leader, which she overheard, being the only English speaker on her team.

After a fierce gunfight and their ascent to our second-floor level, Crystal's true intentions became clear to everyone on my team. When the last member of the Vatican team targeted me and was about to shoot, Crystal intervened, shooting him instead. At that moment, a wounded member of her team managed to escape from the courtyard below.

Confusion overwhelmed me as Crystal surrendered to me. "Whose side are you on?" I asked, struggling to comprehend her actions.

"We are on the same side," she replied. "But I don't have time to explain. We must stop them. Their plans are in motion."

"We'll move as soon as the rest of my team arrives," I replied. "We'll need our whole team to confront the Vatican. It's a fortress. Eliminating Mendolini is crucial, but will that halt their operation?"

"It's crucial but not the only thing we must do," she explained. "Let's go now."

"All right," I said to my team. "Let's move out. We're returning to the Vatican. We'll rendezvous with Abigail and the others on the way."

Gunfire erupted from the hotel's front entrance as we prepared to depart. It was another team, likely dispatched by the Vatican, to eliminate all of us.

"Seems they didn't trust me," Crystal commented, taking cover behind a large ceramic pot filled with dirt and flowers.

This new team was better trained, heavily armed, and not taken by surprise. Crystal and I retreated into a room off the courtyard, eventually forced by the relentless gunfire out into the rear yard of the hotel. We sought shelter behind two sizable trees, lying prone on the ground. Our retreat was blocked by a high wall with a double exit door to our left across an open area. We couldn't reach it in time, even if it were unlocked. Our only option was to engage in a firefight. The wall shielded us from behind, but we were outnumbered from the front.

"That's Tito Galli and Marco Mazza, both top gunmen working for Carlotti," Crystal informed me.

"Who's Carlotti?" I inquired.

"He's Mendolini's head of security and chief enforcer," she replied.

It dawned on me that Abigail, Jim, and Max had arrived and were behind the attacking team while we were in front of them. The rest of my team held command of the second-story hallways.

Amid our accurate shooting and the pressure from Abigail's team, the attacking force was squeezed in the middle and began to diminish in numbers. The Vatican team leader, Galli, and his second-in-command, Mazza, were driven right into our midst.

Finally, we ran out of ammunition and were forced into hand-to-hand combat. Each of us took on an opponent. Galli went after Crystal first, wielding a knife. I thwarted my unarmed assailant with a swift left jab followed by a quick uppercut. Then, I rushed to Crystal's aid, seizing Galli's knife hand with both of mine just as he lunged at her. She evaded his attack but was slashed on her side. Crystal fell to the ground as I wrestled for control of the knife. She began crawling toward the door at the rear of the hotel and the safety of the rest of our team while I grappled with the enemy leader. She eventually reached Marvin, who had little ammunition but could protect her.

While locked in a life-and-death struggle, I heard gunfire approaching. I could only hope it was Abigail and her team. Just as I fell backward with Galli on top of me, thrusting the knife toward my throat, I saw a pistol emerge from the darkened doorway and fire a shot. I didn't know if the bullet was intended for Galli or me. It was Abigail. Her bullet struck Galli in the head just as he was about to plunge his knife into my neck. After rolling him off me, she tossed me a clip of ammunition, and we reloaded our empty guns before reentering the hotel.

Upon our return to the others, they were wrapping up the situation. Crystal was on her feet, her blouse stained with blood but clotting.

"Marvin," I said, "Take her to the hospital. The rest of you, come with me."

"Like hell," Crystal retorted, determined not to miss any part of the action.

"All right," I said with a wry smile. "I won't interfere with my bossy sister's plans."

After collecting as much ammunition as we could from the fallen enemy, Crystal made a brief call from the hotel's front desk, speaking a single word I couldn't hear.

We swiftly commandeered the hotel's airport van, accommodating everyone, and set off for the Vatican. Max took the wheel while Crystal and I engaged in a conversation that the others listened intently to.

"Are you CIA?" I inquired.

"Yes, I am," she confirmed. "That's one reason I didn't want you to join them, among other concerns I raised."

"Did you know the cross you gave me had a transmitter inside it?" I asked.

"No, I had no idea," she admitted. They didn't fully trust me at first.

"So, what was that call about, and what's the whole story here, including your involvement?" I probed.

"I'll start from the beginning, so it all makes sense," she began. "I joined the CIA to follow in our parents' footsteps."

"What?" I exclaimed. "You're telling me our parents worked for the CIA?"

"Both of them," she revealed.

"And you knew that but never told your brothers?" I inquired, surprised.

"I knew it from the day they were killed," she replied. "The men who came to inform us of their death in a car accident were terrible liars, and I suspected there was more to the story. Later, I discovered a box hidden beneath a floorboard in our parents' room containing their CIA identification badges. I was fairly certain they died in the line of duty, so I committed to joining the CIA after you and your brother were out on your own, hoping to uncover the truth behind their deaths and seek justice for them."

"Wow," I muttered, still processing the shock. "Did you find out who was responsible?"

"Yes," she continued. "I gained top-secret clearance, which allowed me to access certain files. After extensive digging, I stumbled upon files deliberately encrypted, renamed, and misfiled to conceal them. When the coast was clear, I retrieved and decrypted those files, discovering records of our parents' murders. An unnamed individual killed them, likely within the agency itself. The files stated there was insufficient evidence to identify their killers, but our parents had reported the existence of a conspiracy within the agency. Other reports in their files indicated that their accusations were never pursued."

"That suggests the conspirators were behind their deaths," I concluded, my voice tinged with anger. "So, your mission shifted to finding out who was behind the conspiracy. But you didn't trust anyone within the CIA, so you went undercover."

"Yes," she affirmed. "Through observation and eventually by earning the trust of one of the conspiracy's key figures, I identified Dunwoody as the head of the CIA conspiracy. But it extended beyond him, and I didn't know who else was involved. So, I maintained my cover and worked toward gaining his trust until he eventually invited me to join their ranks."

"So, you've been undercover without any backup?" I asked incredulously.

"Not entirely," she clarified. "During my regular duties, I crossed paths with the Secretary of Defense and, taking a significant risk, informed him of what I had learned. They had intercepted communications indicating that the intelligence agency of another major power had been infiltrated, and they harbored suspicions about the upper echelons of the CIA. Since then, I've been feeding him information as I uncover it. I'm hoping he has our backs for what lies ahead. That was the call I just made."

"What's the bigger picture of this conspiracy?" I queried. "What if you can't trust the Secretary of Defense? We've gathered fragments but still don't fully grasp the underlying motives and plans."

"Let me summarize the plan," she began. "They aim to establish global Christian dominance, particularly within Catholicism. It's a New World Order they're after."

Suddenly, the letters scrawled in blood on the floor of the charity art auction flashed through my mind—NOW for New World Order. The Rumpled Man was one of the casualties, just like our parents.

"The Vatican is developing a massive biological attack as part of their strategy to decimate a significant number of Muslims, whom they see as a threat to Christianity," Crystal explained. "Their plan involves coating local currencies with a new, undetectable, highly lethal, contagious form of Anthrax contained within microscopic Nanotubes. This contaminated money will then be distributed throughout Muslim countries. The resulting illnesses and deaths will create chaos and paranoia. These countries will suffer millions of casualties and will accuse the U.S., Israel, China, and Russia. This initial attack is meant to trigger a religious war between Muslims and the superpowers—primarily Christian and Jewish nations—on a scale rivaling the Crusades but with modern-day levels of violence. Those initially infected will be those handling the tainted money, who will then transmit the disease to others. The plan anticipates a higher mortality rate among the upper echelons of society due to their frequent money-handling activities. China would subsequently intervene and suppress their vast Western Muslim populations. Given the military strength of Christian and Jewish states, the U.S. and Israel would eventually gain control over the Middle East. The projected death rate among the infected is an astonishing ninety-two percent, occurring within four weeks and followed by waves of the disease spreading across these countries like a devastating epidemic."

"The poor would be less affected, and with these surviving populations, they would be more susceptible to persuasion," Crystal continued. "They would be made to believe that their leaders failed them, that God was punishing Muslims, and that another, more civilized religion could lead them more effectively—namely, Christian leaders who would possess the antidote that the factory developed, creating the illusion of Christian immunity. It would appear as a divine sign."

"Those positioned at the apex of the most powerful countries' governments, placed there over the years by Mendolini, are ready to seize control of those nations. Subsequently, they would become the new political leaders in Muslim regions. The Vatican would govern a less populated world with more easily manipulated inhabitants. Mendolini would have the authority to dictate to the remaining Muslims through control of the antidote and their governments. The Vatican would coerce the remaining Muslims into adopting Christianity by administering the antidote, brainwashing, and economic manipulation. Finally, in the ultimate phase, with the pre-established network within the governments of the three superpowers—the U.S., Russia, and China—all under Vatican control, they would form a consortium overseen by the Pope, the new global ruler. Mendolini would become the immediate successor to the current Pope shortly after that."

"They don't care how many people die," she concluded. "They have the antidote for themselves and those forced to convert to survive—those who become 'saved' in a literal sense."

"So, who killed our parents?" I asked, my voice seething with anger.

"Mendolini ordered it, and Dunwoody executed it," she stated, revealing the long-held truth. Then, I connected the dots to the note "Redbird M" in the report on our parents' deaths—it referred to Cardinal Mendolini as the person who ordered the hit.

"In that case," I declared, my determination resolute, "we're heading in the right direction."

CHAPTER 68 THE VATICAN

The injured man, who had managed to escape during the initial attack at the hotel, made his way back to the Vatican. The Swiss Guards promptly assisted him to Archbishop Santanio's office, and from there, Santanio and Carlotti ushered him into Cardinal Mendolini's chambers, knowing that His Eminence would want to receive his report firsthand.

"What transpired?" inquired Mendolini.

"Our team leader turned against us," he reported. "She shot one of our comrades."

"Carlotti, see to it that he receives medical attention in the infirmary before he soils my carpet with his blood."

Once they had vacated the office, Mendolini turned to Santanio with a grave expression.

"They will be heading here next," he asserted. "We must prepare a surprise for them. Collaborate with the second captain of the Swiss Guard to arrange an ambush right in the corridor leading to our offices. They are rogues, and their desire for vengeance will blind them. They will arrive alone; that's the nature of rogues. Even if they attempt to call for reinforcements, whom would they contact—Dunwoody? Khachenski? I cannot ascertain their exact numbers, but they are unlikely to exceed ten, so ensure we are ready with overwhelming force."

CHAPTER 69 INSIDE THE VATICAN

I suspected Mendolini would be aware of our vendetta, so we hastened to the Vatican without delay. Vincenzo still had the ID card he had filched from the Cardinal's office, providing us with a means of access. I sent Abigail, Max, and Vincenzo to use a side entrance. Splitting up was risky, but the narrow corridors might allow us to strike from multiple angles simultaneously. As we burst through the barricades obstructing our entry, I couldn't help but feel that the resistance was lighter than expected.

"That was too easy," I exclaimed. "We're walking into an ambush. Let's outsmart our opponents, unlike when they fell into ours."

Upon reaching the extended corridor to the Cardinal's office, I signaled the team to halt and seek cover. The Swiss Guards, realizing our plan was unraveled, unleashed a barrage of gunfire. We reciprocated, inflicting casualties upon the guards without incurring injuries. Nevertheless, we soon depleted our ammunition and found ourselves being pushed back. To our dismay, the Swiss Guard had managed to flank us, blocking our retreat. We were on the verge of being outwitted and defeated.

Our team regrouped with Abigail, Max, and Vincenzo, forming a near-back-to-back defensive formation, providing cover for each other.

"We can't afford to give up now," Crystal declared.

The Swiss Guards advanced, determined to eliminate us. As we were teetering on the brink of disaster, we suddenly heard gunfire behind the Swiss Guards, causing them to drop like flies. The sound of shattering windows resonated from nearby offices. Within moments, we found ourselves encircled by U.S. Army Special Forces. The surviving Swiss Guards were swiftly subdued and compelled to surrender.

"You called in the cavalry with that one-word phone call?" I inquired.

"The Secretary of Defense had stationed multiple teams of Special Forces nearby, ready for action in case of trouble," she explained. "The President had even secured advanced permission from the Pope to allow their entry into the Vatican for this mission."

"The President, the Pope?" Jake queried. "Who are you, and who do you serve?"

"I report directly to the White House Chief of Staff, for even the President did not know whom to trust."

At that moment, we noticed Dunwoody and Mendolini making their escape. Crystal pursued Dunwoody while I gave chase to Mendolini. I saw her trailing Dunwoody down the staircase toward the exit.

Out of sight, Crystal confronted Dunwoody in a stairwell, initiating a fierce hand-to-hand brawl. Despite her injuries, she held her ground. Their struggle intensified.

"You killed my parents," she accused.

"They refused to join our cause," he retorted.

"Meaning they were too loyal—to their country," she countered.

"They should have embraced the new world order," he contended. "Global governance is inevitable."

"If they had, I would never have joined, and your scheme would have succeeded," she asserted.

As they grappled, with Crystal weakening, she eventually gained the upper hand, shoving Dunwoody over a railing. He plummeted three stories down the stairwell, landing lifelessly on the concrete floor below.

Meanwhile, I pursued Mendolini into a nearby stairwell, surprised to find that he was ascending instead of descending. He fled like a rabbit flushed from its hiding place, darting uphill. I gave chase.

Upon entering the Pope's residence, I observed Mendolini hastily kneeling and kissing the Pope's ring.

"Father, I wish to confess my sins," he implored. Upon spotting me, he sprang to his feet and dashed down a hallway. I followed in pursuit.

As we raced through the Vatican, the Pope made the sign of the cross towards the fleeing Cardinal. Mendolini descended several stairs until emerging into the Vatican Gardens with me on his heels. Finally, I managed to catch up with him, but to my astonishment, the Cardinal drew a pistol poised to fire. I had discarded my weapon when I exhausted my ammunition and was left unarmed. Given Mendolini's elaborate plans to cause mass death, he had little regard for the Fifth Commandment, so I believed my time had come. I heard a gunshot. World War II veterans often said that you never hear the shot that ends your life, so I knew I was still alive when I heard the shot. I watched as the Cardinal crumpled to the ground, slain by a single shot fired from a distance. Crystal stood in a doorway on the other side of the garden, wielding a rifle. She had displayed her exceptional sniping skills. For a fleeting moment, I wondered when and where she had acquired such expertise.

The dying Cardinal, recognizing that his end was near, had nothing to lose. I asked him, "Why did you kill my parents?" Crystal had joined me by his side.

In a feeble voice, he responded, "They discovered our early plans and began speaking with a journalist. Their deaths were necessary."

His eyes closed, and his head drooped to the side. He had passed away.

I noticed that Crystal's condition was deteriorating due to her injuries and beckoned over to one of the medics who had arrived at the scene.

"I need to check on the rest of my team," he remarked. "Take good care of my sister."

I located Abigail, who was seated with the rest of the team outside Mendolini's office. Everyone had survived, sustaining only minor injuries—a bruise here, a grazed bullet wound there.

CHAPTER 70 ST. PETER'S SQUARE THE VATICAN

About two hours later, Crystal had been tended to by the medics and could now walk. As we exited the front entrance, crossing St. Peter's Square, a surprising sight greeted us—the Pope appeared on his balcony. He bestowed upon us the sign of his blessing. Uncertain of the appropriate response, we waved in return.

Walking beside Crystal, I engaged her in a hushed conversation.

"I'd like to believe he wasn't aware of the conspiracy despite appointing the Propagator of the Faith," I murmured. "But maybe he's not entirely blameless in all of this."

"That's a harsh assessment," she countered.

"I don't trust anyone anymore, you know," I admitted.

"I know that you should consider dating Abigail," she remarked.

"What?" I was taken aback.

"Men can be so oblivious," she remarked with a knowing smile. "Can't you see that she's interested in you?"

"Really?" I pondered her words. I wasn't entirely oblivious to Abigail's feelings. The time might be ripe for something to develop between us. With our mission successfully concluded, is there now an opportunity for a personal life?

CHAPTER 71 PRIVATE JET OVER THE ATLANTIC

On a private plane graciously provided by the President, Crystal, myself, and the rest of my team, we finally had the chance to relax. Jerome had recovered sufficiently to join us for our return flight. We had received word from the President's Chief of Staff that none of the top intelligence agency heads knew the secret network beneath them. As a result, they had all been replaced, ushering in a new era for the intelligence community. I couldn't help but wonder what direction this new era would take—would it return to the Cold War days, pave the way for another global conflict, or maintain the status quo?

"I hope they didn't replace them with their 'next-in-commands,'" I commented.

"Not a chance," Jerome replied. "They've promoted me to Assistant Deputy Director. Retirement will have to wait. The bump in title, pay, and a few more years of work should significantly boost my pension."

"If you manage to stay alive," I added with a wry smile.

"I just found out before boarding that a Special Forces team raided and obliterated the factory—burned it to the ground," Jerome informed us.

"I wish I could have witnessed that," Abigail remarked.

As Crystal and I contemplated what a New World Order under Vatican control might entail, Abigail moved over to sit on the arm of my seat and leaned in close. She felt unexpectedly soft, a quality I hadn't associated with her. Love had a way of blurring one's perceptions.

"We need a society where everyone can trust each other to do what's right and fair," Jenny mused.

"Like that would ever happen," Vincenzo chimed in.

"Perhaps our country's motto, 'In God We Trust,' was intended to remind us to trust in God and no one else," Crystal suggested.

"Speaking of God," I said, handing her back the pieces of the cross she had given me, "I guess it did the job."

The pilot dimmed the cabin lights just then, signaling it was time to rest. Everyone returned to their seats except Abigail. I pressed the button to recline my seat.

"I think I've had my fill of the spy business," I confessed. "Maybe I'll give lobbying a shot. It sounds a lot less complicated."

"Amen to that," Crystal agreed.

The End

* 9 7 8 1 9 6 3 8 0 9 6 7 1 *